PRAISE FOR *SKYLIGHTING*

"The quiet but haunting details in Charles Hansmann's *Skylighting* create a puzzle that, when put together as a reader moves through the book, reveals a portrait of grief and disconnection that sheds light on life's most important questions: what meaning can we find in our lives, in the sometimes-gentle and sometimes-cruel relationships we pursue with each other? Meaning, in this book, comes through in a gauzy, filtered way, delivered through beautiful language that rewards the reader again and again. There is as much importance in what's between the lines as there is pleasure to be had in the story at hand. This book left me reeling, wanting to go back and read it all immediately again!"

—Kelly Magee, author of *The Neighborhood* and *A Guide to Strange Places*

"*Skylighting* dramatizes the days and nights of a grief-stricken man who abandons all meaning. Without pressure to comprehend the significance of other people's words or platitudes, he experiences a strangely alluring purity. Each scene portrays raw engagement—what it must be like to drift along with no concern for revelation or purpose. Every interaction becomes a plunge into stimulus. The result is not meaninglessness but alertness. Work, travel, attraction, tenderness, and all quotidian affairs become weirdly beautiful. From the first page onward, Hansmann's narrator leaves deep wells of subtext. He doesn't insist that we believe or disbelieve but allows readers to fall headlong into each moment's energy. In this way, *Skylighting* is both artistic and gratifying. It should be widely read and loudly admired."

—John Mauk, author of *Where All Things Flatten* and *Field Notes for the Earthbound*

"Like any good novelist, Charles Hansmann isn't afraid to turn his protagonist's world upside down, early and often. As an accomplished poet, he's always got his eye on the luminary bodies in the sky—and his ear to the ground of well-crafted prose. In this concentrated meditation of a novel, Hansmann gets at something still deeper than the nuts and bolts of good literary art. There's a guiding metaphysics here: of loss and secrets, of the ways the living can so easily and so willingly transmogrify themselves into hungry ghosts adrift. There's also the mirror image of that melancholy state: that is, the way memory and remembered promises might offer just the sort of celestial navigation we need to steer our ghost ships home."

—TJ Beitelman, author of *John the Revelator* and *Communion*

"Hansmann's *Skylighting* is a dreamy sphere of a novel written in lovely lucid prose."

—Mesha Maren, author of *Shae* and *Perpetual West*

"*Skylighting* is a delight—a moving, contemplative, and probing exploration of grief and identity, as musical and delicate as a meticulously-crafted composition for a chamber ensemble. The prose itself hooks you; the story delivers the poignant emotions."

—Mitchell James Kaplan, author of *Rhapsody* and *By Fire, By Water*

"*Skylighting* convincingly captures the liminal space of grief. These hallucinatory vignettes, half-asleep and half-awake, render even mundane encounters strange. Loss has knocked the world askew, and we're left with the tilted visions. Hansmann's novella is an astute, surprising journey."

—Erica Wright, author of *Hollow Bones* and *Famous in Cedarville*

"Charles Hansmann's debut novel, *Skylighting*, begins with a tragedy, then moves seamlessly between past and present until time itself becomes a character. Hansmann's narrator, unmoored, drifts from place to place in search for meaning and the hard-earned understanding that 'each person's plight calls out to our own.' The fragility of our existence and potential non-existence is apparent on almost every page. Short, declarative sentences are sometimes enough to conjure entire lives, as in the description of the narrator's parents: 'He taught high-school science and my mother didn't love him. This lasted twelve years.'

Hansmann's clear, concise prose mesmerizes the reader. The ending is spellbinding."

—James Janko, author of *What We Don't Talk About* and *Buffalo Boy and Geronimo*

"In this deeply felt, revelatory novel, a stunning loss sends Nick Nacht on what seems, at first, to be an aimless journey, one in which he feels like only an observer, even within his own self. But Nick's openness to every form of experience—and to insights from various people he meets along the way—ultimately brings him to new understandings about his troubled past and about what his future, shaped by both loss and love, might look like. Throughout his journey, Nick and those he encounters also wrestle with the possibilities and limitations of language, and of attempts to make any kind of meaning with or from it. With the lyricism of poetry and the immersiveness of a philosophical meditation, *Skylighting* entranced me from the first pages. Hansmann has crafted a profound and incantatory work."

—Beth Castrodale, author of *The Inhabitants* and *Marion Hatley*

SKYLIGHTING

Charles Hansmann

Regal House Publishing

Published by
Regal House Publishing, LLC
Raleigh, NC 27605

ISBN -13 (paperback): 9781646036301
ISBN -13 (epub): 9781646036318
Library of Congress Control Number: 2024951450

Cover images and design by © studiochi.art
Author photo by Grant Hansman

Printed in the United States of America

Regal House Publishing, LLC
https://regalhousepublishing.com

for Eileen

and also again and again

ONE

i

We slip down through the clouds to the wakening sea, the sun rising through mist, orange tint, white waves against rolling green headland. At the car-rental counter in Shannon we laugh at the staged poster on the wall—redhaired tykes in ragg-wool sweaters gathering seashells. We keep nudging each other with urchin jokes while the clerk checks options for insurance. Later I discover he has charged us for coverage I would have declined if I had paid more attention.

It is the end of September, the off-season, the rural places empty again.

We are easily charmed. When we stay in a farmhouse everything smells of bread and fresh linen; when we go out for walks the black and tan terrier trots wagging along down the lane. We pay pilgrimage homage to Yeats and McGahern, wander stone ruins deserted except for the blackbirds. We cross pastures of sheep that are shy, pastures of heifers unnervingly curious. We eat jams and scones, drink tea and stout. Evenings we write in our journal, pastiche vignettes in tour-book prose recounting the highlights. Once we hear a milliner speaking Irish on her phone.

Erin insists on a side trip. She wants to see Dunguaire Castle, something she has read. Halfway there we catch the glitter of sea and stop for the view in Drumcreehy. The sideroad rises to a flattened hill, and we watch a small sloop tack slowly up into Galway Bay.

"Sailboats are pulled by the wind, not pushed," I tell her. "It's the wind that has passed the boat that makes it move forward."

The day is cool, the sky clear. "Airplanes too," she says, as one flies over, high up and silent. "They're lifted by the air above them, not by the air below."

I feel gauzy and fluffed, still sleepy. That morning we'd added Ireland to the countries and states where we have made love. I recited them in order, counting as I went, and we ended up on each other's side of the bed.

Everything was reversed: the elbow I used to prop myself, the hand I stroked her hair with. Erin laughed. "It's like seeing ourselves in a mirror," she said. "Everything is opposite. So when you're driving here, Nicko, how do you remember to keep to the left?"

Everything is reversed, and as we take in the view from the hill at Drumcreehy, this change in our lives begins to seem natural. It comes to Erin with the ease of ancestral memory, and to me by willful adjustment, like transposing the bills in my wallet to figure the rate of exchange.

Erin yawns, and watching her yawn, I yawn too.

"Jet lag?"

"Just lazy."

Out on the bay the sparkle of water dims and brightens with a passing cloud; the sailboat luffs, pinched tight, and dips behind the rocks of an island. We go back to our car. I check the map a second time and pull out to the road. Right turn, wrong lane. The crash comes down like a gavel. It is a final verdict, there can be no appeal.

ii

After the accident the days are a blend of shifting amnesia and indelible memory. My thoughts are a blur, a smear, as if I am thinking with the wrong pair of glasses. But my functional thinking is clear, methodical; I make the required arrangements.

Then the panic sets in. My thoughts become desperate.

Erin is gone, all that we had is gone. As if all that we had never happened, as if that interlude of joy was just an illusion. I feel countless lesions scarring inside me, internal marks to mock my survival. Scared panic, almost frantic; then the pendulum swings, and I feel only numb.

My actual injury is only skin-deep. By the time I fly home with the rosewood urn I am already healed. That slash on my wrist where the steering wheel splintered is just a white line. I find it repulsive. It isn't enough.

The flight back to New York is smooth. I keep my eyes closed, lulled by the hum of pressurized darkness. I sleep without dreaming, or in a stranger way dreaming of nothing.

Touchdown wakes me. We roll up to the gate, no wait on the tarmac. All that's left of the Emerald Isle is the attendant's lilting goodbye.

Without any glitch my baggage clears customs. The taxi line is reasonably short; I get into a cab and give the driver my address. He is looking at me in the mirror. But first, I tell him, we need to make a stop. When I tell him where, he turns to face me. A sorrowful look comes into his eyes. "That where you go, mon, that where you go."

I sink back in the seat with my luggage beside me. I hold the urn in a hug. It feels solid, and I feel my heart knocking, like knocking at a door. Not to gain entrance, just for a sounding, a measure of depth, just to come to grips with the barrier that bars me forever.

The only person of value to me, the only comfort, is sealed forever inside the urn. I can't get her back and can't get back the part of me that disappeared with her. I feel an aggrandized grief, a marked distinction, as if I must surely stand out. Why doesn't anyone notice?

Because the mark doesn't show, that's why, the little scar on my wrist is hidden by the cuff of my jacket. Erin has left an invisible imprint. I want it to be seen. I want to open the urn and dip my fingers inside and smudge my forehead with her ashes.

The urge is even stronger when we pass through the gates and drive like a dirge down the long straight driveway. The lawn is immaculate, the trees sedate, the tight-packed graves fading into each other's shadow.

Peaceful graves, and I regret not arranging an interment. I have purchased what amounts to a drawer in a cupboard. The columbarium looks like the mailbox wall in a post-office lobby. When I surrender the urn her ashes are locked behind a small metal door with shiny raised numbers. There's an empty slot for her name, a place for a plaque.

iii

October passes, and the days turn damp and drizzly. I am glad when the trees let go of their colors, the wet leaves plastered to the pavement. I am thankful for the overcast sky, the shortening light, nature in sync with my gloom. The conditions are perfect for suffering.

I go to a parlor in Queens. There I bare my chest for the needle.

"Your parents had this?"

"Just my father."

"A sort of...together-forever symbol?"

"If it was it didn't work. My mother left when I was twelve."

"So you're getting it..."

"For the opposite reason."

It is two rings entwined, in indigo dye, inked on my chest in the sensitive skin that covers the inner corner of my heart. The same tattoo my father got when he married my mother. This was how they had plighted their troths instead of exchanging gold bands.

It was a wedding in the sand, on a Florida beach, a

handful of friends in shorts and T-shirts; one friend a notary public, a teller in a bank, qualified to officiate. With the words, "I give you this ring," they touched the rings in the fresh tattoo.

But by accident or on purpose the rings had a flaw. My mother had picked at the scab on my father's chest before it healed, and the link had broken where the crust pulled away, the skin without ink in the scarred interruption.

A charming story for an abandoned husband to tell his son. And now I am afraid the same thing will happen to my own fresh scab, that I will scratch it in my sleep and mar the connection. I want those rings to hold, to be linked forever. I want no letting go. There's eternity to consider, and while the scab is still healing I wrap up my chest like a mummy.

iv

I give notice at my law firm, where I won't be missed, give up my apartment and everything in it, and book a flight south. It is the weather I go for, the warmth and the sunshine, *la tierra del sol*, not *la tierra florida*. But even so, the flowers entrance me, still blooming so late in November. I buy a pamphlet at a souvenir store so I know what they are.

I rent a one-room apartment and buy a used bike, and time goes by like traffic. The days come up on a heightened pitch, and as they pass the pitch gets lower, like the Doppler effect of a passing car. While the days go by, I stand still. Wherever they are heading is forever out of sight.

The annuity from the accident covers my bills. But with each new installment I feel renewed guilt. Spousal compensation—it is mine by mistake, the insurance I never would have bought if I had paid more attention at the airport in Shannon.

Mistake does not absolve me. I feel as if I have tempted fate.

I am living off her death as if Erin were still with me, and I wear my guilt like a second skin. I try to wash it off in the sea, treading water in the swells out past the breakers. When I wade back to shore and step to dry sand I feel cleansed. But there is always a breeze, and as it dries my skin I can feel the salt tighten.

What winter there is is short. I swim as much as I can. Then the heat sets in, and in June the water's as warm as the air. I like it that way. I don't want to be cooled. I want to pass through water and pass through air by day or by night and feel no shiver.

In July I sit for the Florida bar and set myself up as a freelance lawyer—a hired pen for appellate briefs, trial memoranda and motions for summary judgment. I turn thirty in August, no plans, no illusions. I'm resigned and resolved. Mine will be a subpar life, and I will make it last as long as I can.

My routine takes hold. By day I research my assignments, compose my papers with the careful argument the law demands, and write them up in streamlined prose. By night I'm overcome with grief and mourning. Everything's gone, and I myself am lost.

Erin—always Erin. Our fifteen minutes felt like fame.

TWO

i

Singular focus is the key to success, and success warrants celebration, even if joyless. I win an appeal and treat myself to the salt-rimmed glass. It is the least I can do to acknowledge a job well done. It is also the most I can do, a party of one.

I am sitting in the middle of Linkhorn Avenue. The street is closed to traffic, and the tables outside the Dolphin Bar line up with the afternoon sun. My glass meets the glass of the tabletop, and the light passing through its beveled stem breaks out in a slender prism. I am in no hurry. The caution against drinking alone is misplaced. Sip by sip it is true relaxation.

The sunrays thicken as their slant increases. I hold my drink to the light and admire its citric translucence. From across the patio a man and a woman mistake my gesture and return the toast. I nod to the empty chair at my table and raise my glass higher.

I feel a sweet sadness. A shadow catches the table's edge, and I watch it spread, a slow creep, like watching time. But the shadow's unstoppable only while it has my attention. My fascination is brief, and then I forget all about it. The margaritas have taken their toll, and while I'm not looking the shadow's absorbed into nondescript murk.

The man and the woman carry their glasses across the patio to join me. They sit down at my table, one on each side, and regale me with tales of vacationer hijinks. They have heard about a party, they say, and after several more rounds they invite me along.

The sky in the west is dark, and in the other sky the moon comes up on a beam down the street. Last I looked, days ago, the moon was just getting full. Now it is waning. That fragmented flow takes over the evening.

ii

Music and laughter at walloping volume, a crowded beach house, glistening bodies in low-watt light. Through the whirring motion a girl with chafed skin is looking my way. The rash on her cheeks is feathered like wings, downy, as if something has hatched there.

A few words and we're out the side door to the sand. In the moonlight, beyond the light from the windows, the blur of our shirttails is white and rising, falling and rising.

"Like signal flags."

"What is?"

"Like a message in code."

It's a stumbly joke, and when our legs entangle we fall to the ground as if pulled there. I am reading her eyes as I slip inside her, but her eyes give nothing away.

Their color is all on the surface, as if what we are doing does not concern her.

A clench, an inward cry. She is pushing away, fierce and hostile, the rash on her cheeks like raptor wings riled to a deepening color.

"I'm done," she says, so I quit.

Erin said *intracourse* instead of *inter.* She said it happens within us as one, instead of between us as two. Tonight it is *extracourse*, happening entirely outside of this girl and myself. There's no emotion, not even lust, just perfunctory ardor, as if we are doing it for hire. It is my first time since Erin. I have found a new way to be alone.

iii

I walk home followed by shadows, nothing I can see. Outside my apartment a plane flies over on a rare flight pattern that means strange wind or obscure destination.

A wren whistles and another wren answers. The first wren whistles again. Warblers are waking, but my night is just bedding down. It nestles in my mind as something impersonal, something that happened to somebody else.

As if I have merely observed it; as if the girl were a figment, a stand-in, a make-shift receptacle for a night of need; as if the night were something I paid for.

But the girl is not mine to dispose of. She cannot be so easily dismissed. Bouts of recollection bother my brain, and my brain is nothing if not prescient. On a cloudy afternoon as I walk down the Strand she hails me from a table on the sidewalk.

"Seventeen!" she calls. "But I'm willing to hush." She takes a deep breath and pretends to blow out a cake full of candles.

Her hands are palm down on the tabletop, fingertips arched and spread like a sprinter on her mark. She is sitting with friends deceptively young, tilted back in their chairs and flagrantly smoking. As I turn to walk away I hear one of them shout, "We know where you live!"

A few days later the letters start coming. She recounts each detail, each grain of sand pressed into her skin in our night on the beach. She even gets in the identifying mark: two linked rings, *in epidermal blue,* tattooed above my sternum.

At first the letters don't vary; they unnerve me with their steady reinforcement. I compare each one with the letter before it, saying again the same thing, in again the same way.

Then the letters take an ominous turn. Light pink at first, the envelopes are now a bruised peach. The latest puts me on edge. Instead of a single Forever stamp, six stamps of less value clutter the corner.

Humidity has blurred the ink of the postmark, but I know that it's local, like all the others. The flap is loosely sealed, as if all she could spare were a dab of saliva and a passing lick. I slip a finger inside to open it.

Her message is the same, but today she tacks on the suspense of ellipsis: *I'm still waiting…*

I am possibly the target of attempted extortion, apparently the perpetrator of a statutory crime. Thinking back on that night, I question my first and facile impression. The rash on her cheeks seems less like wings and more like a mask she could no longer wear, the stain from a mask she was shedding but hadn't outgrown.

It looked chafed, her rash, and the thought of it makes my own skin itch. A classic case of psychosomatics, and I can feel it happen, bubbling my skin. Some trick of the mind, an emphatic reaction, breaks out in a pox on my face.

In the mirror it looks like an actor's makeup, painted on, expressive, artistic and planned, there for entertainment. But if the rash is too decorative to symbolize shame, it is still a tacit confession. I wear it like a badge of accusation, a prim red reminder of careless guilt.

As a token of penance my rash is fragile, sensitive to sun. It gets prickly with heat, and I ought to stay indoors. But the sky keeps coming to my window, and the app on my phone shows the tide going out. I can picture the shore getting bigger by the minute, and the vast draining emptiness beckons.

iv

I take a bus to the beach on the outskirts of town. The road traces the shore, and the jitney pulls off at a roadside turnaround, raising white dust on the widened shoulder. Past the low dunes I can see the long breakers glittering far out, a white film of air hanging above them.

I walk through the dunes and down to the hard sloping sand. The surf is gentle close in, just stirring the bottom, and the shorebirds keep chasing the trickling ebb, darting away from the flow. They seem to be eating the water itself rather than picking out insects or bugs.

I wade in to my knees where the water is clear and soak a black hanky, wring it and fasten it over my cheeks to protect them from sun. The handkerchief feels like a mollusk getting its grip. It clings to my rash and the saltwater gives me a quick little sting.

On shore I unbutton my shirt and lie down at the edge of the water. The sun has peaked and will hold that peak for hours. It gives the air weight that feels heavy on my skin, and I let it press down and pin me to the sand. The heat is excuse for escape. I feel my heart crawl away, my chest empty out like a shell.

But the tide has turned and ripples start lapping my sandals. They lift and float, wash in, then start to wash out. I fling them up to dry sand and they land near a boy who keeps throwing a boomerang that will go only straight. A woman is wading through the shallows to fetch it. Out of natural curiosity or childhood drift the boy wanders close and is soon standing next to me. I lower my bandana as he stares at my chest.

"*Mama! Der Mann hat Handschellen auf der Brust!*"

His mother comes up and hands him the boomerang. "Speak English, Klaus." She has cloud-blue eyes and a voice of conflicted allegiance, as if she were cheating on her mother tongue. "English, please."

The boy wipes the sand from the boomerang's blade and purses his lips to mock her. She screws up her face and mocks him back. "*Englisch, bitte*," they say together.

She shifts her hip and adjusts the weight on her legs. Then she crosses her wrists in imaginary bindings and gestures a nod toward her son.

"He thinks your chain tattoo *ist* handcuffs."

I spread out my hands with the ring fingers hooked.

"Not a chain," I say, "*zwei Ringe.*"

She holds up the band on her finger.

"*Ein und dasselbe.*" Her ring catches the sun. "One and the same."

A thin cloud slips over, shading her shadow. She tilts her son's chin to give him some silent instruction. The boy steps back and flings his boomerang as straight as a spear. It punches into the dunes by a tuft of tall grass, and rising from the grass an anhinga flies out with a lizard in its bill. The bird dodges the spray of the spattering sand, loses its grip, and the lizard drops to the ground.

"Geh!" the boy shouts, but the lizard just lies there, small and green in the barren expanse, flattening and subordinate as a shadow, as the shadow of the bird sweeps over.

The boy leans forward, mouth agape, his body impeccably still. I look at his mother. She holds her hand to her brow like a visor and pivots to face me.

"That is instinct," she says, "no escape. It is too far from safety to try."

"Because it doesn't have a chance."

"It only has a chance. Its chance is to stay."

The anhinga banks, raises its wings and lands. It takes a few steps, jerky and awkward, then checks its approach, staring our way as if gauging the distance, the risk we pose, a moment's hesitation, a quick calculation.

I lean back on my elbows. Predator, prey—each of them carries the dinosaur gene, or something like that, and in the end it doesn't matter.

But this is the hunt in its primal display, and the boy cannot hold back. His breath comes fast and his legs kick up. He starts running in place, churning the sand.

"No," his mother says. "Klaus, no. Not to interfere with nature."

"That is the rule!" the boy shouts, ducking her grasp. "*Das ist die Regel!*"

The boy takes off with a yelp. He has a loping run, as if gliding, and the high prolonged leaps slow him. I can see how he struggles to quicken his step, like a runner in a dream. But the sand and the way the boy floats on air reduce him to dreamlike slow motion.

The boy doesn't look back. When he reaches the dunes he picks up the boomerang and starts to wave it, with wild menace, shouting and keeping the anhinga at bay. He dances a gibberish chant—"Hia! Hiawani!"—and keeps tossing the weapon like a juggler, tossing and catching, tossing and catching, till the lizard flushes and darts to cover.

The anhinga rises tall on its legs and stretches its wings, extending its neck, inflating its breast, and the boy steps forward, squaring himself for battle.

A pause: the boy and the bird standing their ground.

Behind them the dune grass brightens with sun. Then the standoff shrugs to an end: an avian shrug, the bird settling its feathers, a baffled disgust as it spreads the full span of its silver-brushed wings. It turns away from the boy and with labored flapping lifts its dark bulk to the air. It flies gangly, ascending and angling.

The boy is caught by surprise. He whirls for a throw, draws his arm back but doesn't release. Instead he just lowers his head, turns the boomerang sideways and clenches it tight in his teeth. Then he drops to all fours by a knobby hummock, sinks low and crawls into the dunes.

"Klaus!" his mother calls, but the boy disappears, his sandy blond hair perfectly blending. "That is Klaus," she says. "He is just like that toy. I have to go get him."

But the boy's disappearance seems to have drawn all the strength from her body. She goes down on her knees, and the sun's new angle streaks color from her hair. A strap has slipped from her shoulder, and I can tell by her tan she doesn't always wear a top.

She shifts the strap and tugs at her swimsuit. "It is supposed to come back," she says, "but not when you hit what you aim."

Her tone is serious, and strangely sad. I reply in kind with a mild correction. "Aim *at*," I say. "In English the target is something you aim at."

She lowers her head as if rinsing her hair in the sun. "But the weapon," she murmurs, "the weapon is something you aim."

V

My own German mother had the same flaxen hair. She was slender and fair, an angular beauty, and seemed like an aunt, not directly related. I liked her remote affection, and I was charmed by the soft insistence of her accent. She learned English in her teens, and her grammar was usually correct. It was only close words that gave her any trouble. She never said *Baum* for *tree*, but the moth at her lamp was always a *Motte*.

My father, third generation, was thrilled to have a wife from his forebearers' province. He was a fan of the open road and put his trust in the route's serendipity. "Off the map," he would say, slowing for a sideroad.

Ours was a quest for natural enchantment, the great American landscape inviting us in, windows down so wherever we went we carried the weather. We were drawn by distance, its transient possibilities, lost in the belief that transformative discovery lay around the next bend. "*Wanderlust*," my mother would say, giving the word its root pronunciation.

I tried to believe that traveling like this brought us together, this scenery we shared, this forward pull toward the unexpected. But my mother remained unalterably foreign. She was never at ease with husband and son, and her presence seemed only an obligatory visit.

With my hand-me-down camera I liked taking pictures of my mother's blown hair. The landscape passed in a blur as the waves of her hair rose and swirled. Each photo was a stroke of futile preservation, as I knew even then, an attempt to hold onto the transience I loved.

My photos were a captured escape that sometimes slipped out to the country beyond. There it was not just moments that passed, but also places. I snapped a pastured horse that galloped alongside us, its gold and blond mane striped in bright sunlight, striped and streaming—not like a flag, but on a continuous current, waving its vanishment into the air. *Ascension horse*, was my thought, *palomino*, and my mind flew out through the thrumming window.

vi

Flaxen—that was Erin's hair too. I watched it emerge from the dress she pulled on the day we married. "Aquamarine," I said, the color of flounce coming just above her knee, the tan knee and pleated teal dress she had bought at a popular thrift store. I matched the spirit of her dress with an untrimmed beard and untucked shirt with a cutaway collar. We dressed in my sublet and repeatedly played UB40's "I Got You Babe." I felt streaks of delight running like neon all through my body. I could see the delight like a sunny cloud floating through hers.

It was hot, and we sauntered, across town and down, to the steamy door of the Municipal Building, which like everywhere else since the Towers went down was now fitted with guards and a checkpoint. No alarms went off and we proved who we were with our law-school IDs.

We were the only ones there without any family. A couple from the Bronx in hesitant English witnessed our vows. Bright scarves, dark eyes, soft laughter and murmurs in Spanish—*mi hermosa esposa, mi querido esposo*—it felt so lusciously sultry. The high ceiling in the waiting room and slow-turning fans made us wish we could elope to Havana.

Ours was one for the books. Minute by minute the day was preserved, though all we would have was its memory. Operator error: by mistake our camera wasn't loaded. It didn't matter at the time because the pictures we took weren't posed and would have been ebullient.

When we popped a cork on the Fire Island ferry, good luck was all we needed. "Good luck," said the woman in the seat across the aisle. Said her lady-friend with the wicker basket and a withering look, "You'll need it."

A sour note, and we laughed it off. We looked over the rail to the approaching shore, where a small crowd waited for the ferry. Luck is other people. We had each other. On this day in history we eloped on a lark of our own.

vii

Back from the beach I slip today's letter into its envelope.

I'm still waiting… Still waiting, but I don't know for what.

There is a knock at my door that sounds apologetic. A neighbor is taking a bus trip Out West and forgot to arrange for her bird. She's already packed, bus ticket in hand—would I do her a favor? Though I barely know her ("Irma," she says, to remind me) I can't say no.

I put the bird on a stand by my window, out of the way and to give it the natural cycle of light. Irma calls it a normal, the cockatiel breed still found in the wild, in the bush of Australia, but she leaves with such fluster she never tells me its name.

At first it is skittish, backs off when I approach and perches in the cage wherever there is shadow. It hisses when I stand by the window, and when I work at my desk it lets out a squawk. Irma said it could talk, but none of the noises are words. The only way to get any peace is to cover the cage with a beach towel.

If the bird is wary, so am I. It has a volatile beak, and I keep my guard. But when I give it fresh greens I can see that its hackles are settling. It softens its screech to a bush call that sounds like someone clearing his throat.

"In for it now," the bird says, with prophetic inflection, and I jot it down. I start keeping a journal of cockatiel wit, and not just for amusement. I think it will show how easy it is to find meaning where none is intended.

A few days later I get a postcard from Irma, and I picture her spinning a rack at the station as soon as she steps off the bus. The card is a colorized photo, neo-vintage, and looks hand-drawn. It shows a pepper tree with dark red berries traditionally used for toothache and wounds, depression and pest control. On the verso she has written in italic script: *Tucson, Arizona—101 at 1:01.*

She has signed it *The Seeker*, with *Irma* in parentheses. From our few conversations I know she sees scheme in chance alignment, mystic intervention in fluke correspondence, even in the artifice of temperature and time. She finds meaning wherever she looks, as if the world were encoded, a cryptograph with a secret message for anyone privy to its signs.

But the Desert Southwest is a long way to travel for such paltry coincidence. Early last week my former bank's electronic billboard showed 92 degrees at 9:20. Typical weather for this time of year, hardly worth noting. But a man at the bus stop asked if I believe things happen for a reason. He started opening vials and pouring his pills to the baking sidewalk. "Because if they don't," he said, "then why do they?"

There was no getting round it. For him the only question is why—why do things happen, he wants to know why even if there isn't a reason. But the only answer we have is how. I watch the cockatiel sidle the length of its perch, one claw at a time. Things happen, as my ontology professor once said, for the same reason that things exist. "We're here, there's this, we've no idea why."

The cockatiel pecks at its image in the dangling mirror, and the mirror spins on its chain. The cockatiel squawks and pauses to preen. Its feathers are gray, clipped at the wing and pearled in a pattern that looks like marble.

"Camouflage," I say, face to face with the bird. "Repeat after me: camouflage."

The bird's feathers lie flat and unruffled. It cocks its head so that only one eye meets mine. "In for it now," the bird says again, and I open the towel to drape over its cage.

viii

I sit down at my desk and take out the draft of my latest vignette. Sweet sadness the mood that brings on Erin. The aesthetic is silence. It provides a lull, and I rest there.

We're naked on our honeymoon bed, out of the pool for an afternoon nap. I've hung my trunks on the handheld shower head; on a hanger that's hooked to the full-length mirror her swimsuit hangs from its shoulder straps. We're drowsy but can't sleep, her swimsuit is dripping. I get up and go over. Her swimsuit and I are perfectly aligned, and my reflected image—legs, arms, head with tousled hair—looks as if I am wearing it.

"'The Merge,'" Erin says.

She always loved giving things titles.

What Erin hated was the opposite of merge: the great separation, the professional disparity—men and women, despite all the gestures and pronouncements, de facto tiered. She complained to me about the assignments she drew in her law firm, that their low-rung status kept her from rising; she said she'd been promised heftier work. In this mixed metaphor of height and weight I first heard her voice sound a chord of vulnerability.

Erin took it out on the mic. She sang *glass ceiling* when "Glass Onion" came up on the karaoke screen. It was Beatle night and we were having a blast, *jurisprudence* as a "Dear Prudence" paraphrase.

There is a pounding in my ears as if somewhere in my building someone is hammering a really long nail. It's the boy from 1-C dribbling his basketball the length of the hall. This is also his soccer ball and punching bag. It is always low on air and rebounds with more of a thud than a bounce. To me it's the sound of what I am thinking: of effort without opportunity, of futile perseverance, of memory coming back with deflated force.

I am done for the day and get up from the desk. Under the towel the bird is rustling the sprig of millet I clipped to a bar. I pull the towel off the cage and fold it, and put it back on the shelf, next to its twin. They're a yin-yang set, towels salvaged from my marriage. Erin had liked the design, the spooning emblem. "Taichi in terrycloth, Nicknik."

ix

I go over to the esplanade and sit on a bench. As I put my arm across the backrest a woman sits down and leans into it. She jumps up from the touch, as if I have groped her, and I stand up too, equally startled. We smile to acknowledge our mutual embarrassment, then she turns and walks off. It is merely an accident of timing.

Flip-flops and sandals: the sidewalk applauds. Since when has the esplanade drawn such crowds? I feel a gnawing at my innards as if my stomach were teething on an iron tine. It is beginning to feel like hamburger time.

I go over to the Hab-or-Nab to have a quick bite. "What'll it be, *extraño*?" I always sit at the bar and the barmaid always calls me that.

"Medium rare, *pepino solo*." My usual order, her usual grin at my high-school Spanish.

"And an order of rings," the woman who sat beside me on the bench says as she takes the next stool. She starts fumbling through her purse. "They have a beer menu here but I can't find my glasses. I was born far-sighted, it isn't from age. Are those for reading?"

She takes the dime-store specs from the neck of

my shirt, a strand of brown hair slipping down to her dark brunette eyebrow. She blinks her green eyes. "Two point five," she says, adjusting my glasses on her nose. "I'm an excellent judge of magnification."

Our conversation is a series of overstrikes. By last call I feel imprinted in an old-fashioned way like paper slowly working through a typewriter.

"Louise," she says, "since you'll want to know my name."

She takes me by the arm as if she were batting left-handed. "I knew you were nice when you jumped off that bench. I bet you open doors."

An understanding has been reached; she simply comes with me. The night is a medley of crickets and frogs. They quiet as we approach and pick up again after we pass.

We turn up my walk, and inside my apartment I drape a towel over the cage to keep the cockatiel quiet. She says she is thirsty, but that sounds like a line, and as I take a favorite glass down from the cupboard I wonder if she has to take a pill.

She drinks the water in the bathroom, the only place in my apartment that is private. When she opens the door, dim light floats out toward the couch where I am waiting. She is naked except for the matching towel wrapped under her arms like a strapless dress.

"I want to make love without taking it off. You don't have to know why."

She pulls the bathroom door shut and goes over to

the window to widen the blind. Partly blocked by the slats the streetlamp looks like a lunar eclipse. I keep my hands to myself as seems to be required. "A moon like this," she says, stroking the strands of shadow and light.

X

If the night is a blur, a gush of wind, then morning comes with sand in my eyes. They are bleary with grit, as if I haven't slept, or have slept with them open.

The woman lies warm beside me. Her breath on my pillow is humid and close, her fingers clutching a dream. I pull on my pants and step into my sandals.

Louise, she told me, so that's what I write, *I'll be right back with breakfast.*

At the Isle Café the cooler is stocked with fruit juice and water. A yeasty smell from the bin behind the counter makes me hungry for a sourdough roll. There is no one at the till.

I hear a flushing sound and a skinny young man comes out from the back too soon to have spent any time at a sink. I put a bottle on the counter and feel through my pockets for a dollar-five in quarters and dimes so I won't have to touch any change from his fingers. I can't get the rolls unless I let him handle them.

On the sidewalk outside I take a long slug of the tangerine seltzer. I have a canteen thirst that drinking only from the bottle will quench. A bum with a bottle in a bag nods in sympathetic understanding. He makes a funny little face and pretends he is juggling.

"This scrap of odds," he says, "ends of the arc."

A scooter goes by, a mocking bird works at its songs, there's a rustle of lizard in the blue jacaranda. The bum counts out three, index to ring, and his eyes get merry.

It's a measurable morning. A dog trots by with its nose to the sidewalk, sniffs an oversized shoe and looks up at the big guy talking on his phone. The big guy leans into the fender of a car. He runs his hand through his hair, fingers spread, as if gauging the length.

I go back to my building for my bike. It has vintage value despite its scrapes and is chained in the hall to a cast-iron brace where there used to be a payphone. Passing my door I hear Louise's placating voice. "For now," she says in an amplified hush. "Don't call me again."

I hurry out the front door. My bike is just back from a bent-rim repair, and I pedal down the street like a boy on an errand. The moon is a waning disc, paler this morning than the rest of the sky. It goes down through the row of solitaire palms and breaks into clouds above the supermarket. They are starting to rise, and the morning air has thinned them.

The A/C in the store is set high, the pineapples chilled in their crates, stacked under a sign that says they have ripened in the field, I guess in Puerto Rico. I press my fingers into one and it feels just right. But I don't want to mess with the cutting and the rind. I buy a chopped-up pint in a plastic container and pick out two cranberry scones. I also buy dish soap, TP and toothpaste, and I'm bounced from the counter with the 5-or-less sign.

Sunlight darkens the sensitive windows. I stuff the grocery bag into my saddle bag and mount my bike. Its riding position is the upright kind. I sit there perched, and as my chest expands I feel myself open to the morning. From the hum of my tires comes the rubbery *Om*—of oneness, or noneness—my appropriated wish to be an Apache, attuned to my visions and flying across scrubland as my pony disappears in the air beneath me. In the enervating sound of my tires I know I can vanish, a component of sky, dispersed and floating.

I am brought back to earth in the long bay of windows on the Isle Café. With the changing angle and early sun they are fully transparent and also reflective. I hold tight to my palpable handlebars as I ride toward their wavering image.

Then I see through it, see through the glass to the round wooden table where the two of them sit: the big guy and Louise. His hands are huge and folded on the table, pushed to the center, and it is clear that he wants her to put hers on top of them.

She turns her head to the side and looks through the glass. Three pigeons fly up as if startled by her glance. Even on wing they leave the impression of a frozen moment.

I look down from her gaze. Under my bike the long brown pods from the blue jacaranda bow and straighten as my tires pass over. Beyond the strewn pods the street lies smooth and rushes to a turn like an asphalt river. I am caught in that current. My bike flies home on a wild ride. When I get to my corner and turn down my street I have enough speed to coast the whole way.

xi

My building is called The Hotel. It's a purpose-built apartment house that never went co-op. A plaque by the door brags a landmark designation for 1933. Even the brass with its verdigris film seems to date from that year.

Thermopane windows were a recent invention. My building was one of the first to install them, one per unit. Mine is hung with a Venetian blind and faces the street. I adjust the slats so that light and shadow in a delicate balance merge on the floor.

It's a soothing mix, but it doesn't last. A truckload of mirrors pulls to the curb and my window is caught in the ricochet glare, a jarring redirection of sun. I go to the window to fix it. For cheap entertainment the stripes in my room swell and contract as I futz with the cord.

I hear footsteps in the hall, knuckles on wood, and go over to answer. Laying my hand on the knob I hear somebody say as if speaking to himself, "You've got the wrong door."

Then the knock comes again, on the door across the

hall. I hear the door open and the same voice saying, "You don't remember me?"

It is not a real question and seems to amuse the silence that follows. I hear the door swing wide. "You," the new tenant says, "get in here."

Mood sits in my room like a smoker. If thoughts were cigarettes, each successive thought is lit from the stub of the last. *Chain thinking*, Erin called it.

I turn my radio on and in the song that is playing the girl doesn't need her nylons and is leaving them home. Somewhere in my building someone is listening to the same station I am, only louder. When the song fades out the DJ announces a commercial-free hour of classic rock. From my radio and woofing through the wall from the radio louder than mine comes an existential song of psychedelic paranoia, reality as decoy and disguise.

I think of that boy on the beach, the German boy. His mother said that a boomerang comes back only when you don't hit your target. His never returned, so he must have been hitting something that we couldn't see.

At last I remember where I set my favorite glass and retrieve it from under the plant stand. It must have been there for days because the drooping philodendron needs another watering.

It is my *other* favorite glass, one of a pair, salvaged like the towels from my marriage. The glass has an etching of green bamboo leaves, just like its twin, and though its transparency is starting to cloud I accept this as proof of vintage authenticity.

I go to the sink past the kitchenette window that I always keep open except when it rains. I am watching it streak in a sprinkling-can pattern when I realize it is time to set my glass down and shut it. As I lock the metal plate that holds it secure I catch sight of my mailman crossing the street. He wears a missionary hat and carries his bag as if it were filled with good news.

The rain slows to a drizzle, a brightening mist. I take the key for my mailbox out of the alligator jar. As I open my door the door across the hall clicks closed, the mist yielding to sun.

"Not so fast," the new tenant says inside 1-H.

I press the key to my fingers and turn it in my hand. It has darkened with use and the coating on its teeth has started to wear.

I open the box for my mail. Another letter from the girl: *I'm still waiting…*

xii

It is almost noon by the time I walk up the broad steps to the courthouse. I've spent the morning reading an old philosophy text and I'm moody in the way I used to be in college. I am briefly entranced on the tread of each step as my toe pokes into its narrow shadow.

The firm where I worked in NYC put great stock in the power of pedantry, linguistic show, pleonastic verbiage. The patter starts filling my head. Law is the art of correction, full of its own mistakes. The truth will out, but only if you go in to get it. Law is the art of convincing someone of something you do not believe, a language best served by rhetorical prolixity.

I spend an hour in the courthouse library, my research lifting from point to point by logic and bright intuition. These are the rays of supposed sunshine, but for me they light up imaginary scenes. I let myself dream about the dress the woman wore when the mechanic shouted catcalls that infuriated her husband.

The husband went home for his gun. Was there time to cool down or was he still in the throes of his angry passion when he went back to the car hoist and shot the man? It is a matter of degree: law judges the temperature of blood.

In legal writing you can't make anything up; it's all precedent and analogy. Law judges our acts whether or not we commit them; murder's a crime on the books, you don't need a killing to make it illegal.

Law confronts, it doesn't shy away. Law takes a hard look, a look that is highly peripheral, indulged from the jaded corner of the eye. Law fosters a scrutiny of strangers, invites our suspicion even as it champions tolerance. Law codifies hope, the triumph of orderly instincts, it sets our expectations. In observance or violation it is something we practice every day.

xiii

On the bus ride home the woman to my right is reading the Qur'an. She has it open to verse 35 in a middle chapter: *Woe unto thee! and woe again!* Verse 36 repeats the message verbatim.

It's an enface text, Arabic and English, and from what I can see, without pagination. Left right, right left—the languages read in opposite directions, and I wonder which way the page turns.

The woman has flattened her lap, like a tray, and her eyes never rise from the book. She has a gentle face and reads with deep concentration, an extended finger guiding her eye down the page.

Block after block as the streets slip by in sunshine and shade she gives the text her rapt attention. Her fingers are tapered, long-jointed. They lift from the page and hover—steady, calm, noncommittal: they are poised to turn the page one way or the other, and I wait on the brink of revelation, the mystery of the page about to unfold.

xiv

The bus jolts, feints to corner, and instead continues straight. A car is trying to pass, but our driver won't let it. He keeps checking his mirror, shouldering turns with exaggerated movement, sliding his hands so the bus holds its course, bloating the lane.

There's a bus stop ahead, but we aren't slowing down. People step to the curb and start to flag us. They've been waiting long enough and aren't going to wait any longer. One man steps out to the street. Our driver brakes and swerves to a stop. When the doors shoot open I step out the back and catch sight of a fender as tires squeal past and a car speeds by in the center lane.

I check the schedule that is pasted inside the shaded shelter: five minutes till my transfer. I put my ticket in my pocket and step back out to the sun. Across the street on my shut-down bank, Dagwood Bumstead, Beetle Bailey and Uncle Duke in colorful spray-paint line the façade with their pockets turned out. The bank is dark and empty, its signboard flatlined and flashing, still sucking power. Beneath my feet are the polka-dot stains where the man last week had poured out his pills. "Points of the lucid," he said, "with no way to connect them."

I let the first bus go by and board the second, sit up front and get off at my stop. The street feels sunken, as if easily submerged, as if the water that would flood it lies close underneath, waiting to surface. My building's a two-story stucco, the apartment designations lettered back and forth along the hall: 1-A across from 1-B. In the vestibule I open the slot for my mailbox. Under a trifold flyer for a tapas bar is the latest installment of postcards from Irma. This time the script is faux Cyrillic. She is now in Sedona. *Red rocks*, she writes, *a vortex of vibes, drinking Corona.*

Irma lives alone without friends, and that's why she asked me to take care of her bird. We'd hardly ever speak, just how-are-you in the hall, but every now and then she would tell me something strange about the pinnacles of time and how they are connected. Irma thinks that the world's an enigma, with a code to be cracked. I told her I find the world puzzling simply because it exists, not because it has hidden meaning. The one, she said, is the key to the other.

"Undercover," her bird says, and I jot it down.

"Repetition," I say. "Repeat after me: repetition."

"Undercover."

"Repetition."

Our staccato exchange conflates with the boy from 1-C repeatedly kicking his ball against the door to his apartment. He is his single mother's darling handful, and our building is a monument to his noise. His ball is a tool of varied use: a pouting stool when he doesn't get his way, a bomb for the ants he has baited with Popsicle sticks scattered on the sidewalk. Painful bravado, touching to watch. His world too is strewn with unease, a litter of things he has to get away from.

Restlessness draws me outside, as it always does, where swallows are hazing the vesper bells, blackbirds tugging a crust two ways. I catch sight of a fender that looks like the one on the car that had jockeyed with the bus. It peels from its spot between a half-ton pickup and economy wagon, rounding the corner with a rubbery squeal.

I go down to the esplanade and sit outside the yellow kiosk. It's closing for the day and its rental umbrellas are stacked inside, its fat-tire bicycles secured with a chain.

On any windy day I can lounge here for hours and watch granules of sand dropping out of the air to the lower pressure in the lee of the sea wall. Today the air is calm and no sand filters through it. The drift along the wall has been here so long it is crosshatched with bird prints.

And yet the air seems impatient, ready for wind. The light is exhausted and cannot hold out much longer. As it starts to fade, the traffic on the strip grows expectant and slows to a drag. These are not cars with specific destinations.

I watch the fender go by the hotel across the street, doubled in the window and finally absorbed in the languorous flow. The car's windows are tinted, and all I can see is the shape of a hand adjusting the mirror or inexplicably waving.

Headlights go on and sunset reflections take cover in the night. Diversion is on the agenda, but it isn't automatic. There are any number of places to go, though I know I might walk the whole length of the Strand and not find a single one.

XV

Darkness, drink, time. I put all three to work and midnight finds me at a glass-and-chrome bar pinned three deep among sunburnt clubbers. The smoked mirror behind the bar is like a mural come to life, the bartenders deftly handling the bottles.

Two women reach through the crowd and with long bare arms gather their drinks from the bar top. One of them wears a strapless white dress with a plain black choker. Her back is partly turned, her face in quarter profile. I sip my rum-Coke and find it easier to follow their conversation than the one I am having with someone named Myrna.

"It's all I can think of," the woman who ordered the mai tai says.

"If that's even what you want"; her friend takes a sip from her Papa Doble.

"If it isn't what I want, then why am I doing it?"

They glide away and claim a tall table that has just been deserted, climb the high stools and settle their glasses without any spill—a testament, I decide, to the advanced evolution of the gimbaled wrist.

"I'm still here," Myrna says. "What are you looking at?"

"Sorry," I say. "Bad memory for names, bad memory for faces."

By mutual indifference Myrna and I let the crowd press and shoulder us apart. Ten minutes later I am standing at the high-top and handing out a fresh mai tai and daiquiri double. The mai tai glass is the same as the glass for my Cuba libre. The woman's green eyes meet mine, but her name escapes me.

"Louise," she says. "It hasn't changed."

I stick with rum-Coke for its crutch of caffeine and we manage to have an engaged conversation devoid of any personal allusion. Louise's hair has a blown-back look, and on the sidewalk outside she turns in my direction for the breeze from the sea. I can see the dim curve where water meets sky, the dark furrows and swells clouding her eyes.

"Let's go for a ride in a cab," she says.

There are plenty of cabs and we are soon getting into one. But when I pull the door shut we just sit there. I'm not sure what she wants. "We have to tell him where to go."

She reclines in the seat and looks out her window. "I don't know the address."

I lean forward and tell the cabbie my street. Louise just watches. As the cab turns around she yields to the sway and leans into her door. Backlit through the window her darkened profile has the stark configuration of shattered glass. A car goes by and I look for her face, but she turns it away to follow the headlights. We ride in silence, the cabbie stops, the dome light goes on, I pay the fare. Louise looks startled, surprised to see me. We get out of the cab and she brings herself back, takes hold of my arm and smiles to acknowledge the effort it takes to escape her own absence.

Inside my apartment she goes to the window and adjusts the blind. "Street light," she says. "I think you like it."

I slide my hand along her hem.

"Pretend you don't remember me," she says.

She takes a favorite glass into the bathroom and comes back out wearing only the towel. "I want to make love without taking it off."

"You don't want me to see."

"As if I have something to hide."

"You don't want me to know what I'm touching."

The towel induces a mix of erotic zeal and tender caress. It has a scent of new fabric, a fresh and clean smell that overrides any fragrance from her body. She is tentative and lustful by turns. By the time she goes to sleep I am lying there thinking how great it would be to have distinct demarcation one day to the next, to have the morning wake me up instead of overtake me still awake. "Louise," she had said, mostly to the pillow. "Next time you'll remember."

xvi

Next time—that would put memory into the future, but the past feels like today.

Eight years ago is as good as now. Eight years ago—the start of a new millennium, the specter of binary chaos. And as it turned out, Y2K was a snap, not worth the scare. By August the 1900s already seemed old-fashioned. There was something so charged about 20 and its trailer of zeros. Two thousand was revved, ready to roll.

"Look at the person sitting to your right," we were

told, "and now look at the person sitting to your left. Three years from now only two of you will be here."

This is the dropout rate, offered as a brag. As if we are embarked on a superior mission where only the noble succeed. It is supposed to make us feel special. But it makes me feel manipulated. I don't like the condescension, the attempt to instill competitive resolve.

And besides, the rate of admissions versus the rate of graduations argues the opposite. Getting through law school is going to be easy compared with getting into it.

Despite my qualms I oblige the speaker, something to be said for compliance, if only to avoid being labeled contrarian. But I can't resist a modest subversion: I look first to my left.

The fellow sitting beside me, who has looked to his right as instructed, is startled to see my inquiring face instead of the back of my head. When I turn to my right the face I meet there remains blank and inscrutable. If the attrition rate is accurate, one of us will have to go.

We are sitting on folding chairs arranged nine deep in rows of ten, an incoming class of eighty-three. The rows bow forward in the middle, like a swelling wave, and my glance toward the center chances on another pair of eyes.

These eyes meet mine and light there. They are framed by flaxen hair. Then the girl lets her eyes drift away. She straightens her collar and winces at feedback from the mic.

The Dean at the lectern fiddles with the mouthpiece and clears his throat. He tells a humorous little story with arching eyebrow. Everyone chuckles, myself included—on a slight delay, somewhere between hearing the punchline and getting the joke.

The school's orientation offers an afternoon tour of the buildings and an awkward mixer with faculty. We stand nibbling on crackers and sipping fizzed punch in compact little groups, giving thumbnail bios with upbeat details.

A professor places my accent, my *inflection* he calls it, within a hundred miles of my Wisconsin town, and a third-year student who is there as a docent is impressed I've scored a sublet within a ten-minute walk. She takes me to task for saying *girls* when I comment that the ratio between sexes seems even.

I am listening to a group that has gathered behind me, the student with the flaxen hair among them. "Erin," she has said, by way of introduction, and from what I make out she has come down from Boston and is staying with an aunt on the Upper West Side.

Some guy chimes in that he lives on Columbus and takes the Number 3.

"Me too," she says, "and then I catch the local."

They agree that they will ride up together. But first he has to stop at the bursar's office to drop off a check. I turn in their direction and catch her eye. We share the same look we shared that morning, brief but slow, not in a hurry.

"Take your time," she tells him, holding my gaze. "I don't mind waiting."

Classes start on the twenty-eighth, the first time in my life I've been to school on my birthday. I turn twenty-two learning the elements essential to a contract. I already know about offer and acceptance. Consideration is the one that surprises me. A promise on its own isn't enough. Both parties have to benefit, both parties have to give something up.

As the year goes by, small cliques form, and Erin's and mine are like tangent circles, they hardly overlap. We have classes together every day, but there is little intermingling. Everyone is red-eyed from study, and dime-store glasses become a fad. The incidental talk is mostly about clarifying how far we're supposed to read in our casebooks. It always confounds us that law-school professors can't state their assignments more clearly.

Toward the end of the year, when our friends pair off for moot-court competition, Erin and I are the odd ones out in our respective groups, and by mutual default become partners. Helicopters straddling state lines—what are the grounds for jurisdiction?

We are given a packet of invented facts and have to parse out the relevant issues. Erin takes it home and works on it first, making notations. She makes a copy so we'll each have our own, and after some telephone tag we meet at the library to discuss it.

The reading room is strangely dim. There are long

solemn tables of book-weary oak. Erin is sitting by a wall that is lined with dark windows. When I sit down beside her she lays out the papers in a disheveled stack between us.

"The feed didn't work," she says. "I had to make the copy by hand."

She neatens the stack and we start to read, going through the copy together. Her notes are mostly lines and bits of punctuation: question marks, exclamation points, underlined phrases and two-way arrows that mean a salient fact could support either side.

We make little checks as we read, keeping quiet except for library whispers. Near the end it's a struggle. The copy machine had been running out of toner and the words are hard to make out. I put on my dime-store glasses.

"For the fine print," I say, "and also the faint."

On the final page the text is slanted, copied at an angle. Three gray shadows, the slender ghosts of her fingers, have been caught in the margin.

"I was in a hurry," she says. "I pressed the button too soon."

The image is eerily intimate. Not suggestive in any way, but a private moment that now is exposed, an aloneness that has strayed outside of her.

I set my pencil down and lay my hand on the page. "There ought to be a law," I say, my fingertips stroking the image of hers.

Offer and acceptance. We lean in, our kiss light, eyes

open. "A law unto itself," she says. "Your wooing is nothing if not subtle."

xvii

I do, after all, go to sleep. Or dream that I sleep. Or imagine I wake up.

Louise is layered, wrapped in the sheet and under the sheet still wrapped in the towel. I go over to the cage and uncover the bird, fold the bird's towel and look out the window. My apartment is only one room, not counting kitchenette, and there's nowhere to hide but the bathroom. Behind me I hear the shower go on.

I take the pitcher out of the refrigerator and pour myself a lemonade. The glass comes to life with its green bamboo leaves against a yellow typhoon sky. It tastes good, so smooth my throat feels like a crooner's.

"Me too," Louise says, coming back out in the clothes she was wearing last night. She has ruffled her hair to dry it, and without any lipstick, no makeup, her plain black choker looks grim. She touches it in the mirror.

"I've also got red and a kind of green blue."

She lifts the glass from my hand and takes noisy sips from the opposite rim. Her lips look swollen, the rest of her face underfed.

"Hungry? I've got rye bread and two kinds of cheese."

She puts a finger inside the choker as her other hand combs through her hair.

"Do you have an extra key?"

"For the door?"

"You might not be here when I come back. I have to get some clothes."

I answer without thinking. "In the alligator jar."

"Where?"

"The alligator jar."

She reaches inside it. "This?"

"The other key. That one's for mail."

She pulls out my spare and holds it to her face, looking into the key as if it were a hand-mirror. "You're awfully trusting."

"And you?"

"Farsighted." She drops the key into her purse and digs deeper. "There they are," she says, pulling out a pair of glasses. She brushes them over her dress and holds them to the light. "Same magnification as yours."

xviii

Louise's hotel is near the cut for the marina, a twenty-minute walk. By the boat slips we sit on a bench in the shade and I set up a picnic on the slats between us. Louise sits with her hands in her lap, amused to be methodically waited on. We watch a bareback man with a salty red beard drink Diet Dr Pepper as he sands out the blisters on his brightwork.

"Have you ever been married?"

"Once."

"A father?"

"Accused. There's this girl…but you don't have to know."

"Sometimes men don't want to know."

"And sometimes we ignore things we should have paid attention to."

The sailor sets down the sandpaper block and starts wiping his hatch with cheesecloth. It's a shabby boat, an old-fashioned split rig, and the masts have fresh varnish only as high as he can reach with a stool. Above that they are peeling.

"What's this," Louise says, "a birthmark?" She puts a finger on my cheek.

"Sun rash."

"You're not very tan."

"Stress rash. It's sympathetic. I knew someone who had it."

"Like male pregnancy," Louise says, "couvade syndrome. I have reason to know."

We get up from the bench, and her thin white dress twists at the waist, the folds hanging pleated at an angle. Last night making love with that towel wrapped around her, she yielded what I thought was her inviolable self, silent, but yielded like a whisper. Trust, I thought, the open heart, and the open wound, whatever it is, lying there inside it.

"We could go to the beach," I say, slipping my fingers into her palm.

But her hand hangs limp; outside her hotel she draws it away. "I'm spending the day at the pool," she says, pointing to the rail along the edge of the roof, "up there. It's treated with salt instead of chlorine, positively amniotic."

"We could swim in the sea."

"Mother of us all. No thanks."

I go back to my apartment and consider spending the whole day there. To keep an eye on the place now that I've given a key to a stranger. But other than my laptop and a half dozen files, a few mementos and worn-out photos, there is nothing I would miss. My life is thought and feeling, inside me, and I find it when I sit at my desk.

I sharpen my pencil and listen. I hold my pencil at attention, poised, fingers alert to the delicate touch, the way they would rest on a planchette. Erin—it isn't her voice I am trying to conjure, just words that will bring back her image.

There's a knock on the door across the hall. I listen as the knock comes again. The door to 1-H clicks open. "I'm back," the voice says. "Did you think I wouldn't be?"

"Back? I didn't know you were gone."

The marbly voice and the scratchy one. There is a moment of silence—it feels awkward to me—and then they laugh, and their laugh has a lot of sex in it.

xix

I walk down to the coastal highway. A line has formed

for the jitney, and I hustle so I won't have to wait. Capacity is twenty, and the bus runs every half hour.

Six boys on bikes come speeding along, and a car pulls over. It's the car that had jockeyed with the bus, the one I saw again last night outside my apartment, and then on the Strand, the one I thought had been stalking me. It slows down and comes to a stop. The car door opens, and the big guy I saw at the Isle Café gets out.

I do a quick count as I step into line. Three girls step in behind me. That makes twenty-one, one over the limit. The girls can't all board, and when they realize this, two of them go over to wait on the bench. The big guy steps in to take the last spot.

Then the boys veer back and skid to a stop. They dump their bikes in the grass, roughhousing and jostling, and butt ahead of the line. With the sun in my eyes, the hazy glare, I see elbows and a flurried commotion. A woman's gone to the front and yanks a boy's collar.

"Don't make trouble," she says in her beautiful accent. "You wait for the next."

I am surprised at the way they acquiesce to her authority. The boys sulk away without muttering a word, and she calmly goes back to her place in the line.

"Okay, Klaus," she says, "we are going to be on this one."

It's a hot humid ride but the windows are open. When we get to the beach Klaus and his mother cater-corner away. I linger behind in the offshore breeze, on the hard wet sand, where the shape of my footprint does not sink in but merely impresses its mark on the surface.

The big guy stands at the water's edge and takes off his sneakers. They dangle from his fingers with long white laces dragging at his feet. His other hand holds a Miami paper rolled like a sheath or a holster.

Eddies of foam flood my ankles. Though the waves are just ripples they work tiny pebbles and sharp broken shells between my feet and my sandals. My skin feels alert in all of those places.

"Some beach," the big guy says.

I look at his face—smooth on the outside, ravaged within—and give him a friendly answer. "I'm always surprised when vacationers find it."

"I just follow the locals."

"You hit some nice weather."

"I'm not exactly here on vacation."

Three pelicans dive into the water in quick succession. For such big ungainly birds they make little splash. The first one to surface tucks its bill down so the water can drain and then tilts its head back to swallow its catch.

"I came down for my wife," the big guy says.

"That's a good enough reason."

"She wasn't too happy to see me. You ever been married?"

"Once."

Even with the sea unusually calm, the wash undermines my footing, sluicing the sand as the ripples ebb, and I have to step back.

The big guy steps back with me.

"I thought I just had to wait it out," he says, "but I couldn't just sit there."

"I guess that can't be easy."

"But I agreed to it if that's what it took to keep her, or at least to get her back. When a woman says, 'You don't own me,' she means a lot more than what you think she does."

The big guy shrugs his shoulders, shoes in one hand, rolled paper in the other, and abruptly steps toward me. He has a surplus of body and seems to have a lot in reserve. He makes the arm with the paper even longer.

"Here," he says, "you want this? I've already read it. Kismayo, Somalia. I almost don't know, are we all complicit? Aisha Ibrahim Duhulow. I memorized her name."

He knocks the sand from his feet. Out over the sea the sky transforms. A high cloud pulls into separate puffs and lower clouds drift in different directions. He sticks the newspaper into my hand and searches my face. But there is nothing he can find there, there is nothing I can tell him. There seems to be something he wants to say, but his face contorts as he changes his mind.

"I don't want to get too much sun," he says. "What's that bus, every half hour?"

xx

Aisha Ibrahim Duhulow—thirteen years old and raped by three men on her way to see her grandma, charged with adultery when she reports it, and stoned in a stadium while a thousand men watch.

Aisha Ibrahim Duhulow: an item in the news…

I take my time on a walk down the shore, and around a far bend the shoreline forms an elongated crescent. There is no one in sight. I look at the sky, the white condensation shapelessly drifting. I think of Erin. "Clouds without resemblance, Nicknik. They don't look like anything else." She stripped off her swimsuit, tossed it to the sand, and swam naked into the swells.

Now I do the same. The water feels like hundreds of hands passing over my body. I feel touched all over, fondled, a plaything of the sea.

What is it like to be a woman? Is this why men want them, because we want to know?

xxi

It's hot walking back to the bus stop, and I fold the newspaper into a sunhat. It gets soggy with sweat, and as I pass through the dunes I stuff it into the gull-proof trash bin.

The bus is parked on the widened shoulder, already boarding. Klaus has his head out the window and is tapping the glass with his boomerang. His mother says, "*Hallo,*" when I sit in the seat in front of them.

Klaus draws himself in and points at my chest. "May I see your tattoo?"

His mother watches intently as I open my shirt. "And it is what did you say?"

"Two rings," I remind her, joining my fingers.

"Entwined," she pronounces, pleased to recall the word. "Like links in a chain."

"One and the same," I say. "You remember."

"And you remember too."

The bus starts up, the dunes slide by, haze drifts in on sheets from the sea. The air takes the warp of old glass, shifting the sky. Klaus turns back to the window and his mother just quietly sits there, absorbing my gaze.

There's permission in her face. She is letting me look, that's all that it is, just letting me look as long as I want. My eyes settle down and rest. I don't have to look anywhere else, I don't have to look away. I cannot get over how calming this feels.

She tilts her head back and raises a bottle. The liquid is clear, I watch it flow. I can feel my own thirst, my longing for that water. Her head tilts further and she takes deep swallows as I watch the slow contractions of her throat.

When the bus drops us off I am the first one out because everyone else has beach paraphernalia. I come down to the bus's tall afternoon shadow.

Standing by the roadside is a handsome trim man with biopsy pittings across prominent cheekbones. One by one the passengers come out with their burden of beach bags and coolers. As Klaus and his mother step down through the door the man raises his hand in greeting.

"Erika!" he calls to make sure she has seen him.

xxii

Walking home I take a detour that leads to the door of Goodwill. In a tangle of hangers toward the back of the store I find a rayon shirt in a sea-green color. I pay the marked-down price and put it on outside, fumbling with the buttons.

The fabric is soft and light. It feels silky, cool, like breeze from a fan. The shirt has been worn on a porch, in a hammock, under an awning leaning all day from sun into shade. I'm aware of perfume, the same as Erin's, the scent of white flowers imbued in a sleeve. I hold the sleeve to my face and breathe in the smell. Perfume in the shirt that mingles with sweat.

The shirt is a relic of another life. I want to touch the person who wore it, luxuriate in that person's scent. I want to reach for her shoulders and hold her, I want to wrap my arms around the memory that's living inside. But the only flesh in the shirt is mine, and I press two fingers to the center of my chest. The vein I touch there is beating to a desultory rhythm.

When I get back to my apartment I find Louise sitting in my chair and fanning herself with my mail. She points at my desk and seems testy, as if she wants to quarrel.

"I put the mail key back into your crocodile jar."

"Alligator."

She rifles through the junk mail and flyers.

"There's also this."

Another postcard from Irma. I turn up my palm and Louise hands it over. Prescott, Arizona, a western saloon with a cowgirl out front spreading the doors.

Louise stands with arms akimbo. "What did you mean *once*?" She sounds accusational.

"*Once?*"

"You said you were married *once*."

"Once only."

"You never ask me any questions. Isn't there anything you want to know?"

"No, there isn't."

"Isn't there anything you want to tell me? Your wife? that girl? this Irma?"

"No," I say again, "there isn't."

I go into the bathroom without closing the door. The cowgirl on the postcard wears a beige fringed jacket with a pattern of miniature broncs, her trousers tucked into filigreed boots. It's a vintage photo from the 1950s, and the cowgirl is probably twenty, though she looks more like thirty in the style of the day. I turn the card over. *Loneliness*, Irma wrote, in ballpoint gothic, *I'd rather touch it like a leaf than shun it like a leper.*

I lay the card down and look at my shirt in the mirror. Louise watches from the bed as I unbutton it. "That's a lady color," she calls through the doorway.

"Aquamarine," I call back, "seawater."

I take the shirt off, and when I drape it on a hanger I can see once again what I saw on the rack at Goodwill: the dress Erin wore when we married, the ghost I once held in my arms.

The disappeared ghost who despite my longing refuses to haunt me in any real way. I am haunting myself, by wanting to be her.

This shirt on the hanger is the height of Erin's shoulders; it seems to fill with her form. "The more you change, the more you stay the same," Louise says when I put it back on.

xxiii

I lie down on the bed and Louise is gentle, her tone reconciliatory. Her face lets go of the strained expression, her eyes soften to a closer focus.

"You're not getting enough sleep," she says. "Because you won't talk. It's keeping you awake. You want to tell me all about it, but you can't, something won't let you. It can wait. You don't have to tell me now."

She seems intent on this, to be consoling, as if she wants to make sure it's done right, a lesson for me, teaching me how to be comforting so I know what to do when it's her turn to need it.

She is tender, touching my forehead, motherly, as if

tending to a child who has suffered some hurt. "It's going to get hot," she says. "Sit up and take the shirt off."

Soothing, her voice, a lullaby, and I drop away fast, a crashing sleep, deeper than dream, dreams too deep to remember. A sunken sleep, without form, a mix of all color, no touch, no image or sound, no tension of absurdities. Aware of being aware, of having that capacity.

And then heat, fatigue, pulling me toward it, a struggle. I wake up on my back, wearing only my shorts. I am sweating. Louise is beside me in only my shirt. Her hair clings to her neck, and the strands of her hair are damp where the collar has caught on her skin and turned under on itself.

Her eyes are closed as if she is talking in her sleep. "Men used to be small," she says. "This shirt's my size."

"You can have it. It buttons from the left."

"You're wearing women's clothing?"

"What about you? When you put it on you thought it was a man's."

Louise gets up and goes into the bathroom, the door swinging closed behind her. That's where she's keeping her clothes, on a shelf in the closet by the towels. She comes back out in a pair of capris, the shirt now buttoned, cinched at her waist with a tie-around belt.

She extends her arm. "Fasten it," she says, handing me her choker.

It is reinforced silk with an oversized clasp. She draws a finger along her throat as she turns her back.

When she lifts her hair I straighten the collar. The clasp has a complicated catch. "Pretend it's a shackle," she says. "Once I am hooked you will never get away."

xxiv

We go over to Linkhorn Avenue, where cars have been banned and the pavement resurfaced in herringbone brick. There is a sign saying PEDESTRIAN MALL, and we walk arm in arm past businesses pedestrians favor. "Ice cream," Louise says, and I buy her a strawberry swirl, and for me two scoops of mint chocolate chip.

It's the milling time of early evening. As we walk past the seating for an outdoor *ristorante* I spot the barmaid from the Hab-or-Nab, still wearing her name tag. She's holding hands with a shag-cut blond at a table by the railing. "*Pepino no solo!*" she says, thumb up, seeing Louise on my arm.

Streetlights come on and the mall starts throbbing to carnival time. A coronet faces off with a sax, running quick riffs and competing in island syncopation. A mime acts out climbing a ladder, afraid of the height. A juggler tosses rings, adding more as he goes, wiping his brow in pretended panic, as if the rings are beyond his control. "How many now?" the juggler shouts out as the crowd sings back his new in-the-air number.

xxv

The sky gets flat and turns to slate, dark slate, then

black as an old-fashioned chalkboard. We count stars walking home, inventing constellations.

"Man-without-car," Louise says, the formation framed by branches. Clearing the tree she names another. "Man-married-once."

Outside my building a jet passes over on a rare flight pattern that means strange wind or obscure destination. It's a thought that enters my mind in words. I have had it before.

"*Once*," Louise says. "I want to know what happened."

The jet banks, heading north.

"Right turn," I say, "wrong lane."

Screened from the moon by the specimen palms, my building is mottled in shadow. Louise counts the windows. "That's yours," she says, "1-G."

It's dark inside, and as we walk down the hall she counts out the doors while somehow reading their letters. "Yours," she says again. "It all adds up, if only you would tell me."

I reach into my pocket for my key, but she beats me to the draw and opens the door with the key that I gave her. When I put on the light the bird squawks. "Say so," the bird says, shifting on its perch, "say so."

I write the words into my journal and cover the cage with the beach towel. I start to undress as Louise goes into the bathroom. She comes back out wrapped as usual in the towel that matches the towel I use for the bird.

My holding back has turned her cold.
"Not tonight," she says. "I want to sleep alone."

xxvi

I sit in a chair, nodding on and off. The darkness seems like a composite word, all the print I've ever read compacting on itself. It enters my sleep like Louise's count-out of the letters on the doors as we walked down the hall. I have a dream about neologisms, but the words skoat free of any meaning.

And then the sky is getting light; birds start singing their surprise. My apartment reemerges from shadow. I'm awake as fitful as I slept.

The air feels tight with congestive breathing, possibly caused by the hint of pistachio in my mint chocolate chip. It is this struggle for air that catches, always catches, constricts my chest whenever I think…whenever I think about the hand held tight on the child's mouth, the quiet suffocation that is almost like dreaming. That was the hand that was supposed to protect me.

I get up and so as not to wake Louise I work by the light of my laptop. Pencil on paper, the letters coming out like stickmen, barely willing to be drawn. This is the reluctant vignette, the fright too far, the memory I don't want to reach.

It starts with an image of my mother, my mother riding away—my mother on the back of some unfenced notion—as fast as she possibly can from the love that corrals her, out of our lives in a cloud of misgivings, so that all of the memories we might have held dear and might have cherished seem false and dreamed up. Even as a man I feel it the way I felt it as a boy.

And this is my father, author of my nightmare, the shouting sleep that rises from primal terror, grotesque phantasmagoria, the breach of a child's trust. My father on a kind of carousel horse, clamped astride those garish haunches, pumping in fettered and fevered motion, silences me with his endless circling, stops my breath with the hand that should have been waving.

xxvii

I go to the window and sit looking out. The light from my laptop reflects on the glass, and what lies outside is overlaid by the image of the room behind me, like a double exposure.

There's a stirring in the bed and I can see Louise turn, her reflection fluffing her pillow, superimposed on the coconut palm. Now she is stretching her arms, fingers to her toes reaching all the way to the street.

As the sky gets lighter the window lets go of the room's reflection. Now all I can do is listen. That is the sound of Louise getting up from the bed, the sound of her towel untucked and dropping to the floor.

Louise is naked, I can hear it. But I cannot bear to turn around. She is ready to be seen, to be touched, to let me know what I am touching, to let me know where it lies within her. But my fingers feel numb, my feelings can't do it.

"I missed you last night," she says. "Why are you sitting here?"

Her whisper is moist, her breath warm in my ear.

"Steed," she says. "Do you want me to ride away?" She puts a foot on the chair like a boot in a stirrup, swings a leg over and mounts.

"Steed," she croons to a rocking motion, coaxing a gallop at both the periphery and the center. It is where we are joined, but she feels like a phantom. The ghost of that shirt still hangs in my mind. Louise doesn't come near; Louise is not real. I feel my body pass through her as if she isn't really there.

"It's her," Louise says, "isn't it? You've no room for me."

She holds me by the shoulders. "*Right turn, wrong lane.* That's what you said. I want to know what happened." She digs her knees into my ribs.

"I don't know how to tell it."

"Start with where."

"We took a trip to Ireland."

"When."

"After our fifth anniversary."

"What."

"What she said."

"What did she say?"

"*When you're driving here*, she said, *how do you remember to keep to the left*?"

Louise nods. "*Right turn, wrong lane.* So that explains your bike." She touches my eyelid as if searching for a tear. "I'm sympathetic," she says, "take me somewhere."

xxviii

A new exhibit has opened called BOOK BY THE COVER. In black metal frames on partitioned white walls, dust jackets and trade-book paperboards are splayed with their pages removed. The covers are authentic, title and author, but the covers are not the point. In 1911 the *Mona Lisa* was stolen from the Louvre. Crowds flocked to the museum to stare at the wall where it no longer hung. The stolen *Mona Lisa* was an international sensation. New records were set for the museum's attendance. Absence had created spectacular presence. As we look at the flattened-out covers, contents gutted, we are supposed to see the essence that is present only for not being there at all. There are clues on printed cards as to how we might do this.

"Nostalgia," one of the cards reads, "from the Greek words *nostos*, meaning home, and *algos*, meaning pain. We ache for what we once knew."

Another card reads: "But what we once knew is missing even when it is here. Basho writes that in his hometown, a bird's call makes him miss his hometown."

We go over to a wall marked FRENCH. The first framed cover is a black-and-white photo of a street outside a cannery. The title is *Rue de la Sardine.*

We both laugh—Steinbeck in translation.

Other walls are marked SPANISH, ITALIAN, PORTUGUESE. "Like the shelves of a liquor store," Louise says, "wines by the country." On closer inspection it isn't by country but by language. Laforet, Tabucci, Pessoa; Bolano, Calvino, Lispector.

"But what is the point," Louise says, "if you haven't read the books?"

The point is that words, for all their content, are not immune to reduction. They can be used as an object, put on display as conceptual art, even when they're no longer present.

Louise is waiting for my answer. A final card, as we are leaving, again mentions Basho. Of an empty cicada shell, Basho writes that the cicada has sung itself away.

Our takeaway, according to the exhibit's curator, is to ponder how a thing's absence is a thing separate from the thing itself.

"What remains behind is nothing compared with what was once there."

A thing separate from the thing itself, like the bear-skin rug Erin and I bought on a car-camping trip the year we eloped. We lugged it home like a catch and spread it out in our den, overlapping the edge of our thinning Persian.

In the mountain store it hung from a wall like a jokey mascot, emptied of what it had been. But when we brought it home it somehow revived, the bear reasserted its power. It had dignity, our respect, and even in socks we never stepped on the fur, always walked around it.

Until once, not looking, Erin stumbled on its head,

and for pity's sake moved it to our footboard. We let it keep watch. "Dark glass, Nicko, dead ringer for the eyes."

These books without their pages—same thing. The vision moves from us to them, not the other way around, but we honor the vision with which they were alive.

It's getting dark when Louise and I return to my apartment. She sits beside me on the floor by my window and we look at the moon. If I am ever to understand her, I can forget about clues to some hidden psychology or revealing insights to her past. What I need is this—this simple sitting in the moonlight without saying a word. It is the only thing we are doing and cannot be stacked up against anything else. It is a respite from significance and its meaningless counterpart.

But Louise still seems provisional, as if some doubt about the world has surprised her, unsettled her, and out of some great misguided guilt or generosity she has applied this doubt to herself. We sit still and silent, but after a while the mood empties out.

"It's always the same," she says, "so for the sake of repetition, take me somewhere."

xxix

We go into the hall and Louise walks ahead while I pull the door tight and listen for the click of my self-locking lock. I don't like that automatic action, the risk of getting caught without a key in my pocket. There are all kinds of places to hide one, but each has a risk I don't want to take.

As I turn toward Louise I remember there's a key in her purse. So far no regrets. But I'm beginning to feel an encroaching tension. She has unusually expressive scapulae, and I watch them register a willed unflinchingness as she looks toward the street through the front door's pane. I continue to wonder what is out there.

Louise redirects my attention. She taps a finger on my arm as we pass my mailbox. "*Nick Nacht*," she reads. "I'm sure there's a story behind that name."

Outside, the palm trees are quiet, no breeze through the fronds. The car with the gleaming fender is parked up the street, other side of the streetlamp. Louise gives it a long steady stare.

"Some people like to watch."

I glance at the windshield. The streetlight reflects straight down on the tint and I can't see through it. We look up at the sky. "Same moon," Louise says. "See how different it looks?" She clenches my shirt at the second button. "Let's go," she says, and we walk arm in arm toward the esplanade, the car slowly trailing.

With each streetlight we pass we walk into our shadows. But the shadows keep stretching, moving further away. They disappear altogether when we come to the lights on the Strand.

At the corner we stop and she looks at me hard. She gives me a kiss that makes me feel bit and spat out. Then she turns toward the car.

"Touch me," she says. "Reach around."

Nothing, it's said, is stranger than the night. Her scapulae register impersonal defiance as my hand slips into her shirt from behind. She lifts her face to the man in the car, letting him know what this feels like.

"Sweetbrier climbing hydrangea," she says.

We step round the corner where the nightlife frays and enter the shorted circuit. We are live among wires, fleetingly finite—then boundless again as we slip from the walk to an alley narrow with trashcans. The curb isn't cut, and the car can't follow.

"So much for him," Louise sneers as the car slides by on the street.

We walk down the swath through the dented trashcans. At the end of the alley a neon sign repeatedly blinks two letters: *WI*. Louise grabs me by the belt.

"Let's go in."

She keeps pronouncing the word in time to the flash: *WI*. "That's the question," she says, "the eternal question. Just an alternate spelling. That's wireless without the fidelity."

We take stools at the bar and order the advertised beer. Her swig is all wrist and the bottle set down foams up through its neck. I throw back my head for a long cold guzzle. The beer shoots to my brain and I like what it does there.

People on the dance floor are grinding, that slow suggestive sex simulation. Then they shuffle partners as if dealing a new deck. Pairs regroup into clasping threesomes, some women sitting out. They start dancing to a song called "Sandwich Cubano."

"I've seen that in the city," Louise says. "There they call it 'Brooklyn Bridge.'"

She leans back on her stool and her knee jerks down as her heel loses grip of the rung. "My marriage felt like a job," she says. "It felt like…if you make love even though you don't want to, is that rape? Shouldn't he have known?"

"He didn't know how to read you."

"But did he have to be so totally illiterate?"

She hitches her heel on the rung. "I wish I was shipwrecked like you," she says. "Life as an island, a poem instead of some stupid story."

"Life as an island," I say. "I never understood why Crusoe didn't stay there."

The dance floor gets crowded, the dancers throbbing and miming cues from the lyrics. They do it in a stylized way that looks more choreographed than raunchy. I lay a twenty on the bar and we slide from our stools.

"I'm yours," Louise says. "And if you want to, you can be mine."

I feel those words at the bottom of my heart, the very bottom. But the feeling doesn't last. When we hit the open air I can tell once again that nothing has touched me.

XXX

In the morning Louise wakes me with a bombshell.

"You should know I have a daughter."

"A daughter."

"She's two."

"And your husband…"

"Agreed we would consider her his. I wish I was shipwrecked like you."

"You have a daughter."

She stalks off to the shower. "Is this where you go moral on me?" She gets into the stall and turns on the water without testing it first. "Or just where you grab a convenient excuse?"

Louise has a daughter—and I know I can't do it, can't shatter that young girl's home. Or am I just trying to protect the boy whose mother broke free and left him so willing to be pitied? the boy whose mother deserted him and left him forlorn? There is no fast rule, though each person's plight cries out to our own.

"Driftwood," my father had said, my irresolute life under discussion, "when you're not sure where you come from."

I had decided to quibble. "You mean not sure where I'm going."

"I mean where you came from. You know what *nicht* means, don't you?"

"Of course."

"Your mother said *Nicht Nacht.* Bit of postpartum delirium. I thought she was talking names, and I had them put that down—*Nick Nacht.* I didn't find out till later that she was talking paternity. You are, apparently, *not* a Nacht."

So then I knew. It was not just the cancer that was eating him. Not just my presence, but the very fact that I existed. I was the book he didn't want to read.

It was raining that day when he told me, the day before he died, and nearly ten years since I had last seen my mother. The tawdry disclosure was something I did not have to know. It felt like another betrayal, his final contribution to the soured feelings that had gone off between us. I looked out the window and felt the weather in my eyes, sheets of downpour, but I resisted even then the notion of a sympathetic sky. Because weather cannot be held accountable.

Because only we can. And it's only any good if we hold ourselves accountable in advance, before the act, not absolving ourselves with contrition. It's only any good if we let accountability have a say in what we do, not just make us sorry for what we have already done. It's only any good if it makes us live up to the honest expectations we have set for ourselves.

And so a new day, a new morning.

One towel covers the birdcage, and the other towel hangs on the bar by the shower. The matching pair of yin-yang towels, the spooning emblem of opposites that Erin and I had found so delightful. I stand immobile between them.

When Louise shuts off the water I close the bathroom door as gently as I can. I can hear her towel off, much ruffling of hair. Ten minutes later she comes out and tosses her towel on the chair.

"I can leave," she says. "I can simply leave them behind."

"Louise—"

"But you can't let me."

She packs quickly and hands me the key as I walk her down the hall. The car pulls to the curb and the familiar fender slips into shade. Louise opens her purse and drops her phone inside, and her shadow disappears as she ducks through the car door.

I go back to my apartment and leave the door open. As the car drives away all sound turns off. I sit facing the door, my back to the street, and wait and listen.

xxxi

Irma walks in in soundless shoes, the kind that have harmed no animal to make. Part of greening the planet is traveling light—she sets down her small duffle.

"I'm back."

She steps into the room with a noticeable effort to lift up her eyes. I am impressed by their size but they won't hold a color. They seem raw, abraded, peeled of the layer of cells that are supposed to protect them.

We gently shake hands. Her movements are slow

and deliberate, as if she were taking them one at a time. I nod toward the cage.

"You've got a feathered friend there who'll be happy to see you."

She smiles at this, and if her spirits were low they now seem to rally.

"Did you teach her any words?"

"Her?"

"You didn't know? Cuckoo's a girl. That's why she's still got the pearling."

"Camouflage," I say. "It wasn't on purpose."

She laughs, a little uncertain. I don't mention my journal, my flailing thrust with pointed pencil. Let her have her beliefs. Point proved, point forfeit: point dulled and pointless.

Irma looks at the cage and pulls off her hat. Her dark red hair is like something metallic, like the stain of some ore. She seems to have come to this world from deep inside it, as if she'd been mined. She looks worn, fittingly so, her face like dry land, etched with erosion and wildlife trails.

"I hope you didn't mind."

"Taking care of Cuckoo?"

"The postcards."

"They were fine. I like your calligraphy."

"It was such a long way," she says, "and so much of it alone."

The lines in Irma's face from sleeping on the bus have started to lift, a deep smoothness in her skin rising to the surface. I ask how she liked the Painted Desert.

"Like ruins," she says, "frescoes that have faded."

I laugh. "The ravages of time."

"Yes," she says, "*the long slow making toward today.* That's how the tour bus described it." She smiles. "I just wanted to be there," she says. "I could have done without the narration."

I lift the towel from the cage and lay it on the chair beside the towel Louise dropped there. The bird holds back when Irma offers her hand, turning away. Irma holds out a finger but the bird won't hop to it. "I guess I'm being punished," Irma says. "It takes her a while to warm to me again."

She reaches for the towel. "Let me launder that."

It's the towel Louise used.

"Please," I say, folding it neatly and handing it to her, "a present for Cuckoo."

After Irma leaves I toss my cockatiel journal into the trash. Whatever it proved doesn't matter. If meaning doesn't exist it shouldn't take such pains to pretend that it does. It shouldn't promote such perfect illusion.

In my drawer I find Erin's first passport, surrendered for the one with her married name. I stare at the official punch-hole that rendered the passport invalid. The punch-hole is right on target. It pierces the laminated gloss at the base of her breastbone. Marking the spot, the exact point of entry, to guide that shaft of lorry metal.

xxxii

It is checkout time at the hotels along the beach, and I walk down to the Strand to witness the exodus. There are cabs all over and mounds of matched luggage stacked in a lineup of bellhop carts. A boy keeps spinning the revolving doors and dashes out as a woman loses hold of his hand. "Klaus, wait here!"

I wave and walk up. "Are you leaving?"

"Yes. We go home."

Her husband is watching the luggage, handing out tips, charmingly polite to the uniformed staff. Even in shorts he keeps strict control of the loading.

"Well then," I say, "*auf Wiedersehen.* I hope you come back."

"Yes, like the boomerang."

"No," I say, "not like the boomerang. I hope you come back."

"Then you hope I have missed what I aimed at."

"*At,*" I say. "The last time you said that you didn't say *at.*"

"You remember."

I smile. "And you remember too."

She looks at me then the way she might have looked at some boy when she first started dating. She touches her fingers to my sleeve, and her husband turns toward us.

"Erika!" he calls. "*Jetzt müssen wir gehen.*"

She collars Klaus and leads him to the car. "I am happy your rash is over."

xxxiii

Lawyers are trained to identify the issue, to formulate an argument in support of either side. To make a case through inference, even if the facts are merely circumstantial. Things don't just happen, the lawyer insists, there's a limit to believable coincidence. That's on the one side. The other is that things happen by chance all the time.

Outside my building my day continues its race toward resolve. As I come up the walk, sunlight to shade, consequence without ceremony is thrust into my hand. It's a personal delivery, a dark-peach envelope.

"I'm still waiting," the girl says, saving me the trouble of opening it.

"But waiting for what?"

"Not waiting for long."

"But for what?"

"For your worry, waiting for your worry to grow, like your own special pregnancy."

"And here you are."

"I didn't even have to lie," she says, "because you never asked me my age."

"Are you really seventeen?"

"None of your business. Are you scared or just curious?"

"Are you really pregnant?"

"Not anymore. Are you sorry?"

"Yes, I'm sorry."

"Because you know you're in trouble. And you know you're going to pay for it."

Mercenary, I remember, that's how our encounter had felt, as if for pay instead of for passion or pleasure, soldiers in battle without believing in the cause.

"Is it money you want?"

"To make me a whore? Just go."

"All right, I'll go in. But if—"

"Not in. Away. Pack your bags, Buster."

"Pack my bags…"

"A guarantee," she says, and I feel my skin prick. "This is God's mercy, not mine. God took six days to make this world. His mercy gives you six to find a new one."

"And you are the angel of mercy?"

"I'm the avenging angel. Right out of *Revelation.* And here's a revelation for you. Six days. If you're here on the seventh my mercy turns you in."

xxxiv

Her ultimatum is like cutting a cord. Just like that all the tension collapses. The girl wants only to cleanse herself. I'm a residue she wants to wash off, toxic to her skin. She wants to take something back that she lost, or something that was stolen.

And whether I am the only thief or just one thief

among several, she's intent on making me pay. Joint and several liability—that's the legal term: you're responsible for all the damage that's been caused if you've caused any part of it.

I travel light—a briefcase, a backpack—and like the cicada I sing myself away.

Uber to the airport. Up the stairs to security. And after the rack of rereleased novels I enter the echoing concourse. I find my gate and doublecheck my departure. The monitor shows an indefinite delay; the announcement overrides it; my flight takes off on time.

It feels like escape, but to what?

It feels like dust beaten from a carpet. It feels like a record expunged.

I buckle up and sit with good posture. I have both feet planted on the flying floor. Wind bucks our lift above the great savannah. We rise toward the band of overcast sky. I look out my window at elemental landscape: strip of earth, watery heaven, the empty air between.

But the air is deceptive, pocked with pockets. Turbulence grips us. We're shaken like a cocktail. Then it's calm as we enter the high-lying fog. I go back to my book. The centenary celebration of Ian Fleming is upon us, and I've got the new edition of *Casino Royale*.

Two thousand feet up we break through the clouds and a peaceful sunlight brightens my page. The plane is coasting as if it were still, and the clouds now form a horizon below us. In the blue sky above them the two-thirds moon looks dented and bunched—imprint on a pillow.

"Troposphere of dreams," Erin would say as wisps of cloud scattered about us.

"The skylight zone," is what I still answer, embraced once again in the floating bliss.

THREE

i

The city I have chosen is arid and coastal, with pockets of jungle humidity. From the plane it resembles an amphitheater with suburbs running over the rim. It opens to the sea, and glare on the water makes it seem as if the sea were a stage—an empty stage with dramatic lighting.

The plane banks and I close my spy book. Chapter seven likened gambling to a play in which actors create their own roles. Chapter nine explained how an agent's code name reveals certain aspects of character.

The same is supposedly true of penmanship, and I'm convinced I can work the dynamic in reverse: alter my writing to change who I am. I open the book to its flyleaf and practice signing my name. Longer stems, more rounded loops—this is the role I have decided to play.

I've rented a place in a modest sector not far from the college. The neighborhood seems both grubby and scrubbed, a little of each, with a secondhand bookshop around a far corner. The shop is maintained in meticulous order and caters to a polyglot market. Its aisles are labeled for the reader's language rather than the original language of the writer.

In the city I have chosen, English is common, and on the ENGLISH shelf among familiar classics is a book that will suit my purpose. It is a slender volume of translated lyrics and aphoristic prose, nuggets of thought that do not demand continuous attention. I can dip in and out as I please. I can use it as a prop.

Families at leisure, children at play. A reader quiet among them intent on his book does not arouse suspicion. He goes unnoticed, like scenery. On my bench in the square I am as much a part of the afternoon park as the limestone fountain and statue.

I am here just to watch. This is as close as I will get to life without illusion. It can no more be mine than the life of a monk or assassin. It's not that illusions are false and can't be attained. By their very nature, belief gives them validity.

Erin and I were orphaned adults, we were twinned that way. Her feelings were mine, and mine hers. We entered each other's memories and assumed those memories as our own. I was the frightened young girl startled by the hummingbird, she the terrified boy charging through the dark on a runaway horse.

We would lie in bed enclosed in the night and feel in our hearts the beats-per-minute of thrumming wings, and touch in the air the dark wooded menace of low-swept boughs. It was a full exchange, nothing held back. I kept and transferred all of my memories to her, she kept and transferred hers to me. With Erin's death

I carry both of our memories into the world that she'll never see, the park I am sitting in now.

I look up from the page as if resting my eyes from reading. I'm surrounded by children, by attentive mothers, by portable tables spread with refreshments, colorful blankets for crawling babies. One mother, taller than the rest, wears a gypsy skirt accentually high-waisted. She walks back and forth, one end of the square to the other, like in an exercise yard. I watch her turn, and like verse upon verse her pacing makes me forget my page.

It is only as a study that I see her, a specimen, and this does not make her real. I suspect she is caught in circumstantial confinement, and I imagine ambitions thwarted, humdrum domesticity, a bedroom dulled by perfunctory affection.

Tipping my book for a better view, I see that it isn't that simple. She is taking the air in sycamore shade, out for a stroll of unhurried laps defined by the length of the park. And she is free of all fetters, unconstrained by my bland description. At the end of the square, where she always turns back, there is a part of her she lets continue, into the street, toward the sky. What strikes me is that I can see it so physically expressed, as if voices were calling.

Calling me into the night she enters my sleep the way a sailboat enters the wind. She is powered by the force that is moving against her. She tacks through my dream with zigzag momentum. I am drawn the way a sail is drawn, pulled by breeze, filled and taut, into its passing.

And then the sea deepens to the darker oblivion of doubtless sleep, the pressured depth that light and breath can't reach, where pale anaerobic creatures reenact the fossil crush, where the dreamer's sole awareness is snuffed, his impression pushed into mud.

ii

Night unsettles my longing for clarity, like a stick poked into sediment. But when the darkness clears, order's restored, and the days come and go with familiar regularity. They occupy a space of no consequence. Arguments shouted in the streets' squat shade resolve to farewells as the shadows lengthen. The pavement heats and cools, and even slow bicycles blur their spokes. Children look up and peer into faces that one day will fade from their memories.

This is the city of my dreams, and the fact that it exists makes me question that distinction. It is cobbled and plastered, awash with light. Day after day the sun holds steady, or it shimmers, watery, an abandoned shell submerged in the sky.

And the sky is a swirl of birds and trees, utility poles; of kites and shoes tied by their laces and flung to the wires; a whirl of wind and eddies of litter, of dust and last year's leaves. It is a catchall sky, and later and later each afternoon the moon comes into the day still waxing.

I am done with the practice of law and walk through the city with unbuttoned sleeves. I am looking for work, and this seems to be the costume. Work that will be no different from what I'd be doing if I weren't getting paid. I want a job that doesn't require my being there, a job that scoffs at studied skill and accumulated know-how.

At a portable kiosk serving ices and ades I see a notice on the window for a counterman, someone to don a white apron, tend to the booth, put ice in the cups and money in the till. The kiosk is one of a dozen, in the heart of a row by a downtown park. It promises anonymity.

The work is manual, mechanical, out in the open for everyone to see. Such is freedom, at its very basic, the unhidden act, the honest expression, day after day without subtext, nothing to conceal and nothing implied. A day with no agenda, no one to convince, no argument to present, no negotiation of terms. The very thought makes me dizzy with elation.

Traffic speeds by on the boulevard, then stalls—quick gusts cut short, a fan unplugged. I feel fumes on my face and breathe the exhaust. This toxic exhilaration is all that I want. It overwhelms me with pleasure, a love for the world. I can play my part and not pay tribute.

Down the edge of the park the light is dappled. I cross the street into solid shade. My rooms are above a grocery that advertises food from the troubled Near

East. I have a table and a double brass bed, a spare set of sheets, and a bath that is lit by a skylight. The glass on the skylight is coated with dust and layers of what I assume to be pollen, though it seems that the sky itself leaves a film.

The skylight is fixed in place, it doesn't open, and lying in the tub with the suds to my chin I can watch dead leaves caught in its seams in illusory flight as clouds pass over. The light sets me adrift. I lie quiet and immobile, at one with the steam and dim translucence.

I float away to a memory that's only a dream, a dream that is launched by loss. My imagination is faithful and true to what I have promised, Erin in the ache of my heart.

It's a delicate dream, a young girl's memory. It's Erin's memory, and she loves to dance. It's a memory of likeness: she's as tall as the table. It's a memory of mimic: seeing the table's shimmed leg she lifts her heel. It's a memory of passage: on tiptoe she finally can see out the window. It's a memory I hold as my own, because with Erin's death I am the memory's sole depot.

The water chills and my shivers ripple. Imagination is fickle. The image of Erin gives way to that mother I saw in the park, the trailing hand that her child's hand could not quite reach.

She is the mother who gives her child no access. Not so much how she fills the role as how she appears not to want it. As if cast against type by a quirk of fate or errant decision.

Even the vision that attracted me—her pacing, her height, her high-waisted skirt—in embellished replay now seems like disguise. Her turning step at the end of the square, her backup pivot with out-flung arm, made it clear she was maneuvering more than her body.

I feel the tug, the strong draw, but the reverie has a mind of its own. I am wary and keep my distance, coy within my own imagination. I am shy with the conjured image, pretending my interest lies elsewhere, just as I had on the bench in the park with the book on my lap.

I do not determine who I am. I am not myself to any greater extent than I am anyone else. Even within my own self I am only an observer. I am the witness who does not contribute. My dreams day or night are brusque, unwieldy. They refuse to perform to my bidding, and I have to accept what they bring me.

iii

After the bath I am eager to warm myself walking. The chilled water I rise from is so out of keeping with the general heat that it seems artificial. Like so many things that demand our attention, the heat has a presence distinct and separate from everything else. It holds in the city even as the lights go on and people come out in clothes that try to ignore it. It is the single reality that can't be altered.

This is the city of my dreams, a sadness fulfilled, and I feel great relief to forsake feigned joy, to look deep into ache and longing. Everywhere I walk the streets are arush with longing, the sidewalks loitered with longing. The sidewalk cafes are crowded with longing, and the longing sits back and lounges. No one disturbs it by trying too hard to get what he wants.

I drink an ice tea at the portable kiosk and ask the girl who serves me, with a sour little smirk, whether she likes her job. She seems to think I am offering some other employment. I point to the sign that is taped to the glass and tell her I am thinking of applying.

"Fine for me," she says, "but you're not the type."

As it turns out I am exactly the type. The work is just what I want—easy and mindless. Or so I would once have described it. But though not difficult, it is minutely intense and demands my full concentration. The focus of the job is the product; customers can fend for themselves.

The cutting board is mahogany, bleached through the years with citric stain. The acidic juice has eaten away at the softer wood in the grain, so that the surface of the board, once smooth, is now corrugated. To get a clean cut I have to make sure the knife comes down on the ribs.

The lemons are like fingerprints or snowflakes, no two alike. They have to be selected for the knife, not just picked at random. And the cut has to go exactly into its preordained slit. It is a pushing away that eases the lemon in half, and a fulcrum shift far back on the blade, a gentle downward pull, a final twist that severs it.

With the essence of lemon teasing the air, one by one the wasps home in. They dart back and forth, attentive little eyes, and watch my every move the way a jury, rapt, once hung on every word as I pretended to address them with passion.

The job is devoid of camaraderie; we work our shifts alone. There is either high attrition or a lot of part-timers, and I rarely see the same person twice. I keep looking for the girl I bought the ice tea from, but she never has a shift either side of mine.

One day I walk home through the large central park and see her standing on the outcrop that is hooked like a thumb in the bowl of the city. Her gaze is upward, intent on the sky. I climb the stepped path that leads to her perch. The sky is clear, not a cloud, nothing but the unrelieved blue. She hears me approach but doesn't turn around.

"Yes," she says, "if you ask do I remember you."

"What if I ask what you're looking at?"

"The moon," she says. "You can see it too."

It is a mushroom moon, tipped up, a white shadow.

"The moon by night is boring," she says. "By day it's something to look at."

"A gibbous moon—"

"But even by day it is nothing to speak of."

She takes me to a bar that has tables on the sidewalk. We pass on through and take a dark booth inside at the back. I sit on the bench across from her. Something has started, and it seems incumbent on me to keep the thing going. She isn't much help finding anything to say. We are indirect and elusive, but as we sip our drinks our eyes meet.

"I'm Nick."

"Jaci."

She spells it in the air with her finger—*J, a, c* in rapid succession, then a slow-motion dotting of the *i.* She slides over on her bench to make room. I push my drink across the table and come around to her side. She takes another sip and stares straight ahead. "We don't have to talk," she says. "Especially if it's only made up."

It is the same in my bed, as I soon find out. She is passive in a way that requires invention. I wonder whether she's shy, inexperienced or easily mesmerized. Or whether what we are doing is merely better than doing nothing at all.

"What's the difference?" she asks.

"Between what?"

"The moon," she says. "When the sky is blue it's surrounded."

"And at night?"

"At night it's just a hole in the sky."

iv

I am eventually assigned the breakfast shift and have to open the kiosk at dawn. There is light in the sky above the boulevard's trees, but it darkens again when I turn on the light above the cutting board. Our sign says FRESH and we mean it. I spend the first half hour squeezing oranges. I've been told to extract all the juice I can get, even if it means a drop of bitter rind. The sweetness is strong enough to bear it, and depending on the cultivar, sometimes improved by it.

My customers are dressed for work in an office, but there are always a few from demolition crews, construction and even sanitation. The coffee stand and the one that sells pastries and all kinds of bread are busier than I am—they have the aroma.

As for myself, I don't drink juice or rev up on caffeine. Dates and figs from the fruit stand give me the wake-up I want. I save my coffee drinking for later in the day, as a way to relax in the late afternoon, and I always follow up with a single glass of wine.

My favorite café has tables outside the Museum of Indigenous Peoples. One day the mother I saw in the park arrives in a cab and climbs those steps with a packet in her arms. She comes back out empty-handed, and I get the impression these are regular deliveries. My afternoons now have a purpose.

On the third day of vigil, streaks of steady rain keep me close to the wall beneath the awning. The waiter brings my wine and the wind picks up, and I have to go inside. She is seated toward the back near the alley entrance. Even sitting down she is tall.

There is an empty chair at her table, and she pushes it out with her foot. "Don't think I haven't noticed you," she says. She motions toward the chair and I sit down.

"Men are men," she says, "but when they are not men, sometimes they are creepy, sometimes they are boys. They have eyes, but they do not have words. Are you creepy, thinking what you would do to me, or just a boy, too shy to say hello?"

I reach a hand across the table. "I'm Nick."

"You were mooning," she says. "You had your fantasy. You just wanted to look, you wanted to keep your fantasy pure."

Her hands are wrapped around a cup of coffee. When I accept what she says, nodding, she lets go of the cup and offers a down-turned palm. It's an old-fashioned gesture, the back of her hand presented for deference, my own hand turned up to receive it.

"Selena," she says. She brings the coffee to her lips, and when she lowers the cup the moisture's still there. She looks over the cup at my wine. "You drink alone?"

My fingers can still feel the warmth, the ceramic warmth her hand transferred to mine. I reach for my glass and the warmth dispels. "When I have to. Will you join me?"

Some private amusement comes into her face. "You decide."

I order a single glass and set it in the middle of the table. Her eyes don't bother to look at it. "Now we have chess," she says, "without the board. Chess with only one chess piece." She moves the glass sideways. "I suppose you think we take turns."

I drink from the glass and set it back down between

us. "Chess," I say, "or anything we imagine. Let's say this glass is a word we don't know and we have to determine its meaning."

"A foreign word," she says. "We have to translate it. Translate it into what we understand it to mean in the language we speak. Because this is what I do. I translate."

She points toward the museum. "Native texts, the ancient ones. Where nothing is continuous. A fragment here, a fragment there, and in this way the ancient text completes itself. But it's a different matter when the language is newly discovered. I'm making the case for scratches to qualify as alphabet. I'm speaking figuratively, of course, or quoting the term used by my detractors. Naturally I make assumptions. Vocabulary, grammar, syntax. All in the service of context. These are the tools, to make it intelligible.

"But this, this is an isolated language, with its own set of oddities. Some words have two values, and some verbs have no aspect, so that things that happen just once also keep happening forever. Purpose—I ask myself: what is the purpose? Because language is not different from us. We want to translate our incoherence into something we could mean. Something we might believe. An identity, shall we say. This is what, if we are exalted, exalts us."

I tell her I disagree, that purpose is what limits us. "It tempts us to jimmy the proof."

"You think purpose undermines the truth?"

"I think it chokes imagination."

"And imagination is…"

"Abruptions, thoughts breaking off into—"

She holds up a hand to stop me. "Finish that glass. Get two more."

I drink the rest of the wine in a gulp and bring two new glasses back from the bar. This time I set a glass in front of each of us, lined up, straight down the middle.

"Drink," she says.

I take a sip.

"Use your imagination. All of it. All of it at once. Imagine how thirsty you are."

I finish it off and she nods at me as she pushes her own glass across the table.

"Mine too," she says. "Imagine you are me. Because now I am curious. I want to see what your imagination looks like."

"You think you are teaching me a lesson."

"And what would that be? A lesson about violated space?"

"My thoughts are my own, I can do what I want there."

"Thoughts can contaminate."

"Thoughts about people aren't people; thoughts about people are not even things."

The wine in me has gone to her advantage. I drink the glass quickly.

"Good," she says. "Now repeat the lesson."

When we leave it is dark. The rain has stopped, and

under the streetlights the sidewalk's immaculate gray, washed hard, as if the rain has poured out a more durable concrete. Small shadows crouch in the alleys, a cat crosses the street to avoid us.

"I am fond of cats," she says, "but they have always been afraid of me, even though I just want to pet them. And what about you?"

"What am I afraid of?"

"Or what do you want?"

We stop. "What I want. I know what I want. I want to be unencumbered."

"You already are. Maybe that's what you're afraid of."

V

In the morning I wince at my reflection in the mirror. But I don't have time to improve it or to fix how I feel. Jaci invited me to visit her, and I have to dress quickly for the last morning train to her suburb.

She described it to me in a kind of set piece. A suburb, she said, where the streetcar tracks are still embedded in the cobble and the beach gives way to low dunes and high bluff. Because of the fog that is there every morning, the scrawny vegetation can make do without rain. There is lushness too, she said, but only in pockets of tiny discretion, where the fog tightens up and pulls in on itself and waters the ground with big drops. Except for the fog the sky is what the locals call clear, but only by comparison. It is never deep blue, there is always something pale—wan air, thin but distinctive.

As I leave the city the sky is immaculate as the sea. Through the train's smudged window it has the faraway blue of a dome. But as the train speeds along, the blue rinses out, and above Jaci's suburb the sky films over like a milky eye.

Jaci said she would meet me at the station. But when the train pulls in, the platform is empty. I wonder whether she's had a change of heart—our one time in bed was hardly propitious. Then I hear a shout and heels hammer down the wooden stairs from the street.

"I wasn't sure you were coming."

"I wasn't sure you would meet me."

We are both nonchalant, as if to imply no commitment either way. But I want her to like me, and Jaci seems equally determined. We get into her car and our kiss feels worried. The physical connection is all that we have, probably not enough, but I don't want to lose it.

The top is down, the rush of wind an excuse not to talk. Salt is in the air, the smell of pine and eucalyptus, the scent she has dabbed on her neck.

We drive through straight streets of mixed use. Some have trees, some are walled, and the old part of town where workers once lived has been transformed into premium real estate.

The car slows and comes to a stop. "This was my school. I was third in my class and could have been first. Except for foreign verbs. I balked at learning more than three tenses."

She has parked in the shade of a spindly tree outside the front entrance. Her hands are on the wheel and she worries her nails back and forth across her thumbs, clicking their edges. "*Did* is as good as *had done*," she says, glaring at the door.

I brush my hand along the fine leather dashboard. The vertical surface has a darker tone, less faded by sun. The leather feels like the hide of a calf that has lived its short life on milk.

"But now I'm in college," she says, "second year." She laughs. "Business, I'm all business. I've had it with language and the silly fancy things it thinks it can say. I've had it with nuance."

She takes me to a house that looks abandoned to the weather. There's an empty lot beside it, rusted junk in the weeds, coiled springs and obsolete appliances. Between the house and the road is a drainage ditch and a makeshift bridge leading to the door.

We enter a small room. There's a rickety bed pushed up against a wall, lighted by a window on the opposite wall. It's a filtered light, the sun coming through a scarf that is strung as a curtain on the glass. A woman is sitting on the bed, and the pattern of birds on the scarf is projected in shadows all around her. As the woman looks up, the birds fly into her face.

"This is Lucine," Jaci says, "my poem."

The woman leans back, looking to the ceiling, and the shadows of the birds settle dark blotches on her cheeks. Jaci begins to recite.

Your neck scarf hung across the sunlit window
Raises on your sheet the dark birds flying
That you have unknotted from your throat.

We are quiet as a pin. Jaci seems lost in reverence for her words. Lucine hardly breathes. "I work backwards," Jaci says. "Instead of writing poems about things I have seen, I stage little scenes about the poems I have written." Her eyes are shiny. "Backwards," she says, "the echo and the reflection, then the sound and the image. I put my title at the bottom instead of at the top. This one's 'Delicate Anguish,' and it ends like this."

She takes a small breath.

Thrush breaking dawn with learned identity,
Blackbird letting go of night in song only,
Your dream lets go the colors you have slept to.

She takes me by the hand and we go out the door. "Anyway," she says, "I'm sorry I invited you. We have guests this weekend, and I have to take you back."

In the car she has nothing more to say. She gives all of her attention to the wheel, the intersections and downshifting to slow us. But I am not content to drive to the station in silence.

"You're all business? you've had it with language? and yet you write poems?"

"That's what poems *are*, complete rejection of how we think and how we think we should say what we think. Poems are just…just that."

When we get to the station she walks me down the

stairs. At the bottom, when I step to the platform, she stays standing on the last step above me.

We kiss like that, at different levels, my face turned up the way a woman's usually is. It's a tightened kiss, and her lips seem thinner, as if they have phases like the moon. I can see the moon in the high whitened sky.

vi

The white sky has become a fascination, like a weathered stone whose engraving can no longer be read. It has drifted to the city from the suburbs, and I often find it hard to look away. It seems as if the sky has cleansed itself of clouds, and the clouds didn't go away easy.

It would be false and pathetic to say that the sky casts a pall; if anything, our streets and windows are brighter. The sky is its own reflection, and when birds fly over they look like the shadows of birds over water.

On my walks through the city my vision is willing to make things up. My mind has released in peculiar ways, and reining it in exhausts me. The fatigue is a kind of catalyst; it makes me receptive to whatever stimuli come my way.

In my apartment it's the same. As I lie in the tub in a drowsy state, a lethargic mood, like a snake's digestion, crawls head to toe through my body. My eyes feel heavy, but I can't make them close. The image in my eyes is not what is there in front of me. It is a self-induced trance, and limited for this reason. I can go only as far as I already know how to go.

My dreams about Selena continue.

She is a phantom of missed opportunity, of things not done. I see her in a calculated way—for her importance to me and not for who she is in herself.

These dreams are a breakthrough left hanging, a source of understanding, a scourge of misunderstanding. The parts of myself that elude me I believe can be cornered and caught there.

But I feel unfaithful. These dreams should be about Erin. No one ever made any sense except her. Yet here I am clutching as her image slips out of my grasp.

Selena is a mystery; that is what has captured me. Be she forever unattainable, there is this. For how can we possibly know ourselves if not by what we can never know of another?

"To perceptual dissonance," Erin said, raising her glass for a toast. We were sitting high on a terrace, where big pots lined the bluff instead of a railing. We looked out at calm sea over dark red geraniums, then leaned and looked down. Wave upon wave was breaking close in, sunlight on the water shattering to thousandths, surfing to shore. Not calm at all.

The emotional dissonance I'm feeling now exposes me as a hypocrite. Dreaming of Selena I think I'm unfaithful to Erin, yet I have no compunction about sleeping with Jaci.

I see Selena again, on my way to the kiosk. She is riding in a cab, as graceful as ever, and it comes as a shock when she loses her poise as the taxi bumps over a section of ruts. I wouldn't say her head bobbles; there is nothing so vulgar about her. And it wouldn't jibe with the image I have come to insist on. Her head just moves without conscious intent, subject to the laws of physics rather than her own volition. She'd been looking down, probably reading, a book on her lap. By the time the street is smooth again her head is lifted and within her control. She says something to the driver that makes him turn toward her and shrug.

The difference between seeing Selena in the cab and dreaming about her in my reveries is that standing on the sidewalk I feel like a voyeur, as if I have stolen her image, whereas sailing with Selena through my reveries, all guards down, defies the usual strictures of possession. Nothing in those dreams can exert any hold on her, nothing can restrict me, nothing can hold us accountable. We are free not to be who we are.

With Jaci my thoughts chase their own tail and never catch up. She is far too elusive, too quick for sloth rationality. I have to rally myself to try to understand what she has already passed through. I can never figure out where she's going until she is going somewhere else.

She's alive in her work, while my own weak efforts bring me nothing but shame. I'm embarrassed to think of my collected false starts, the scribbles and cross-outs of disjointed fragments on tattered pages in the drawer of my desk, the stranded phrases that fail to cohere.

vii

Jaci's house is a rambling two-story on a wide and deep yard with enormous trees that siphon all the water from the lawn. Their roots spread out as far as their branches and leave the grass parched in a drip-line pattern. It is my second visit to her suburb. Jaci has picked me up in the city and gives me the history as we drive. Nothing dramatic in her story, but I look for the telling detail. She is so careless with clues they tumble out without consequence and never give anything away.

Jaci's house is a hundred years old, in her family the whole time, and though slightly remodeled, none of those changes is recent. From the curb its appeal is ramshackle charm. I can tell it has seen hard use, oblivious to preservation, a dogeared book.

Her father she describes as an impresario. On a small municipal stipend he arranges an annual season of community plays. Adaptations, translations, and sometimes one of his own. The locals and expats all know English, and this is the language he uses.

His money came through marriage, and though he never strove to enhance this fortune, "neither was he profligate." This inverted phrase closes off any questions the information gives rise to. If selective disclosure is what Jaci is going for, she's hit the right note. I wonder about her mother, but can't phrase the question in a way that does not sound prurient.

Jaci's father greets us at the door. Carefully casual, gracious, kind: he makes an immediate good impression. But he is also a bit preoccupied. He tells us he's been working upstairs and has just come down for a glass of water. He holds out the glass as proof.

"Lemon water," he says, pointing to the slice that is floating on the surface.

He is handsome, has strong features, with hair swept back in a way that suggests he used to wear it longer. He still looks like the man in the photos on top of the piano, taken, probably, ten years apart, and the woman beside him has also aged well. In fact, she seems to have aged in reverse, and the woman in the first photo might not be the same as the woman in the second.

In a photo facing the front of the piano, Jaci is wearing a school girl's uniform and carries a satchel. She looks about eight, the photo a dozen years old. I assume the boy beside her is her brother even though they bear no resemblance. They stand side by side in a protective aura that seems to exclude the rest of the world.

I want to pick up the picture of Jaci and the boy, to comment on it and question her. But Jaci's pause when I glance at the photo makes me feel as if this is expected, and the answer already prepared. So instead I ask, touching the piano, "Do you play?"

"We all play," her father says, and I nod to acknowledge whatever he means, to let him know that it hasn't been lost on me.

Jaci follows her father upstairs. "The *Oresteia*," she says when she comes back down. "He's putting on the whole trilogy." She hands me a copy of the Vellacott translation. "He wants you to read it in case you come to a performance. You'll enjoy the show more if you're not just following to find out what happens."

We go out to the patio and spend the whole day there, in canvas sling chairs with a wicker table on the flagstones between us. Jaci has laid out three pencils, sharpened, and jots down notes on a pad as she works through her textbook. She turns the pages of the book with thoughtful care and also makes notes in the margins.

The paperback *Oresteia* is a Penguin Classic with a golden death-mask pictured on the cover. The face in repose with quiet eyes seems to have glimpsed its underworld soul. I skip the introduction and start reading *Agamemnon*. Sentries keep watch, but there's no welcome home for the conquering hero. Clytemnestra can't wait, she's dying to kill him. She's got a new lover and her motive is double: disposal of the husband she has now replaced and retribution for the daughter he sacrificed for favorable winds. She plays false, pretends love before striking the blow.

The play's a revelation. I had a Latin minor in college, but never read much of the Greeks. The action in Aeschylus stems from an attempt to placate the gods; in Ovid it's more by intercession of the gods: a boy wrapped in amorous embrace blends with the body of the nymph who loves him, a dead wife dies a second death when her husband flubs her rescue from the afterlife. Illegitimates in the *Metamorphoses* are the offspring of gods. But claiming this paternity is not without hazard. Phaethon scorches the earth on his fatal ride when he loses control of the sun god's horses. I took this to heart when I read it in college. I was finally learning to drive, belatedly, and I knew I was a menace, I lacked the right focus.

I also lacked focus as a student. In Comparative Lit I liked Kafka's fragments better than his stories, partly because they were shorter. By haphazard signup I garnered the credits for a philosophy major. I was an ardent fan of Camus and embraced his cure for absurdity. There's no meaning to life, he tells us, and our freedom lies in looking for it. I took his advice and searched for this meaning in books that were never assigned, writers who managed to wander around on the fringes of intelligible thought. I looked for meaning on the water, in the sailing dinghies at my college boat club, where I would sit at the tiller and by adjusting the sail could negotiate with the wind a compromised direction—a reconciliation, I thought, of fate and free will.

I found feelings and ideas, pleasure and interest, but meaning never attached.

viii

Like rote recitation, the days go by without emphasis. I keep a lookout for Selena because I want to make a second and better impression. I embarrassed myself that night drinking wine while it rained. I don't understand what she meant to prove. If she was initiating me into some rite of awareness, I'm sure I didn't pass the audition.

I'm sitting at my usual café and think I see her. It's just a glimpse as the door of the museum is closing. I've looked away for a moment, distracted by a conversation at a table behind me. "No they don't," the woman said, "alphabets represent sound." When I turned in their direction her companion responded, "But sound travels better."

It is the second conversation I've overheard in two days. The first time the keywords were "fraud," "hoax," and "fake," an indignant tone that implied authentication was not forthcoming. I didn't turn around that time and now I'm not sure the voices are the same.

I finish my coffee and wait for my wine. The waiter doesn't come and I go inside. There sits Selena by the other door. She motions to the chair across from her.

"Nick," she says, "you take a long time to figure things out. You're going to learn nothing by obvious surveillance, like a secret agent whose cover's been blown. You don't really see what is here. You just suppose. This makes you transparent. It is painful to see through you so clearly."

"But isn't it the same?"

"What is the same?"

"With you. With these scratches, this ancient text you claim to have discovered."

"*Claim*. I wonder where you heard that."

"Let's say I am guessing."

"It's a question of exploitation."

"You promote your translation, but the original you keep hidden."

"The text demands reverence. I am protecting it against the diminishers. Who would argue it into its opposite, that the text is not what it proclaims to be, or does not say what it purports to say. If I don't produce the source they can question only my claim to its existence. They cannot distort the text itself."

"Verification requires proof."

"But these are matters of the heart. What we believe relies on an honest interpretation of the proof. What we deny leans into our bias."

"But those scratches you described, like bird prints you said. What if they're exactly just that, accidental, bird prints that have fossilized? A random so-called alphabet totally devoid of any message, of any intended meaning."

"As some have said they are, bird prints, a joke at my expense, the implication being that my brain is of comparable caliber.

"But bird prints scratching out a creation myth that acknowledges its own uncertainty? A theogony of believable gods who question their own divinity?

A founding myth devoid of heroics or platitude, eschewing sentimentality? A moral outlook at odds with the strata and core economics that are the basis of our own?

"The very notion is subversive. And preemptive. These are the writings of original intent, if that's your standard. And if they're just bird prints, literally just ancient bird prints hardened in mud…well, impressions can serve many purposes. And let's say it wouldn't matter. In my view they annotate the scrolls."

ix

Moon by day, that disappears in bright sun, that vanishes when the sky clouds over.

I am hardly writing anything at all. My abruptions break off into fragments. So secret is my secret, and twofold: no one knows I am writing, and no one knows I am not. I am hardly even reading. And when I do read it is only a few pages at a time. I have only a few books, and I often read the same few pages. They seem complete in themselves. I am reading the movement on the surface, and that is enough, no need to go deep.

My connection with Jaci has mysteriously lapsed, and I'm not sure what to do to get in touch with her. Her school in the city has too many buildings to stake the place out.

But she knows where I live and I have told her she could always stay over if her classes run late. I have given her a key. She is a challenge to my grief, to my resolve to be monkish, or at least to be devoted to the memory of my marriage, to be wary of opening my heart to another.

I have a storage room that is empty, a kind of glorified closet, that I offered to set up with a desk and a cot. One day I hear her key in my lock. Despite all the time that has passed I am not surprised to see her. Jaci is twenty, and however worldly she seems, she is also still strange with youth and innocence. "Let me see it," she says.

My closet is six by eight, a little cell of seclusion, ideal for the student. It doesn't have a light or an outlet, but I offer to run an extension cord under the door. She insists on paying a small rent and makes me promise that I will not object if friends come over to see her.

We set out for the street stalls in search of a cot and desk and lamp. Over the next few days she adds a portable turntable and two crates of old records, the only thing she collects. She likes to imagine the houses and apartments where the records were played.

"And when there's a scratch," she says, "I wonder what caused it."

The friends she brings over speak the careful student language that doesn't suggest caution so much as an integrity for getting things right. They are willing to promulgate outlandish views but do not want to misrepresent them. Jaci uses the room mostly as a day place; she rarely spends the night. That changes and she starts sleeping over, always on her cot, though sometimes she first shares my bed. On one of those nights she accuses me of suppressing curiosity.

"You never asked about the pictures."

"What pictures?"

"You saw them, the family pictures. It's been bothering me, why you never asked."

"I think they were a plant. You wanted me to ask."

"Pretend you are curious."

"It must be your mother."

"Whom I never knew."

"The younger one your stepmother."

"Who never warmed to me."

"The boy your half-brother."

"We were close. She took him with her when she left. Tomas was five. I was eight. I'd been teaching him the alphabet, our initials. I showed him his T, my J. He couldn't see the difference. He said we were twins."

X

It is the season of flux. The sky above the city keeps changing. It is crosshatched, like a fine net, as if we are looking at the sky through a sieve. It is grainy, a picture of the sky in poor resolution. Jaci looks up and scowls.

"If I knew it was going to be like this," she says, "I would have stayed home."

She gets moody and starts spending more time with the door to her closet closed, listening to those music-hall records. They are bawdy or sentimental, romantic or clever, set to catchy tunes.

At first I think they are just an entertainment, a release, a little break from her schoolwork. I think by the spread of books I have glanced on her desk that she is diligent with her studies. But Jaci seems distracted, and when she comes out to use the bathroom I sneak into her closet and try to find out what is bothering her.

Entrepreneurial Mind is closed. I push the book aside and move the coaster off her note pad to see what she has written. Eight lines in her usual neat pencil, easily legible: a fair copy, it seems, except for the one overwritten erasure.

Nothing reigns unchallenged, rock outcrops
Bowing to the pines.
A boy, a girl, and may they
Slip the clouds' loose shadowy chains.

Jaci claims her words rise out of nothing, her poems a manufactured reality, fanciful. This isn't a claim I can give full credit. Something in the world must have triggered them, at least in part. Ideas are born of image and feeling, and borne on words that convey this. But with Jaci it is different. It is not so much what she finds in the world as what she finds lacking. And this is why her poems unsettle me. They seem to undermine or maybe pass through her own understanding to reveal what her heart can never know.

I read the second stanza:

The task of else allows
Plastic staves in wicker baskets,

A glass wall, a cloth pail,
Waves leaking from the garden faucet.

xi

One night Jaci says, "We need a complication. What if I showed up with a stranger?"

"And this would be?"

"A special guest, he's an older student with worldly appeal who has gone back to school after a dozen years of travel and adventure."

"That would make him my age."

"And he's smart enough to play it low-key, emotionally safe, immune from the turmoil of students who have just turned twenty. Myself, for instance."

"And his age…"

"Gives him an advantage."

"And he's studying…"

"Economics. But not out of interest in policy or theory. He thinks it will help him manage his father's fortune, of which he will be the sole heir."

"A cardboard figure."

"Exactly. Safely two-dimensional."

"He needs more humanity."

"He's also taking courses in comparative religion."

"But he's ambiguous as to why."

"It isn't clear whether he believes that similar themes among different cultures debunk or validate the stories on which they are based. Or whether religion has some practical use, some exploitative potential that is suited to his purpose."

"When can I meet him?"

"We were only supposing."

Jaci has memories I will never know, and she will never have access to the memories embedded in me. Her fabricated stranger is an attempt to find something of ourselves in an imagined other. Or she may be conjuring a more suitable boyfriend, if boyfriend is what I am.

Erin sometimes mentioned lovers from college, but she never compared us. One boy was musical. I heard all about him, Jimmy, but I never felt jealous. He was bluesy on guitar, she said, but couldn't play up tempo. But he could make his fingers hurt, on those strings, and every note he'd make her feel it.

xii

I am invited again to visit Jaci "at the house," and the train ride out feels as if the city comes with me. This is because the sky stays the same the whole way. That whiteness I first encountered in Jaci's suburb has spread to cover the whole route.

Repetition is the mother of change. Like the first time there, I'm not sure Jaci will be at the station. But as the train pulls in she is standing on the platform, holding her skirt down as the slipstream puffs it.

I step off the train and we stand face to face.

"On the level," I say as we kiss.

In the turbulent air as the train pulls out, her skirt once again puffs and billows. "I know what you mean. Don't look so surprised."

This is our first standing kiss without the distortion of her standing on a step. I can look straight ahead right into her eyes. She is exactly my height.

"What do you want?"

"What does anyone?"

"I want the one I love…"

"…to be the one I love."

Lucine is waiting in a park. She has picked flowers and flowering weeds, and has laid neat bunches on one seat of a teetertotter. She is dressed in a gossamer shift, her aura ethereal, and her skin is perfect for Jaci's purpose, pale as a blank piece of paper.

The light in the park, shaded by trees, is the same as the light that filtered through her scarf the last time that I saw her, when the pattern of birds on the cloth was projected all around her and finally all over her face. It had seemed then like a kind of suffering, her appearance today intentionally transcendent.

Jaci begins to recite.

She imagines her weight in flowers,
Handfuls of dandelions
To balance the seesaw,
A park full of daisies lifting her

Here Jaci pauses, her voice suspended to let me

know she has stopped midsentence. Lucine holds the flowers from her face, as if she doesn't want to breathe them. She carries the flowers before her with a held-down grasp, as if she were keeping them from floating away.

She walks to the swing and sits on the hanging seat. Her free hand takes hold of the rope and she starts to pump, holding the flowers aloft as if she were pumping to reach them. She leans back and looks out beyond the crossbar.

Swing past the trees.
More than imagine she sees,
In the rows beyond the playground, bouquets
Commemorating stones.

"'Posy,'" Jaci says, "that's the title."

I turn around without further prompting. With the sun setting behind it, the cemetery looks like a field of clouds rising on the hill. It seems to have risen from the words that Jaci recited, her poem appearing before my eyes on the power of Jaci's recitation.

Jaci holds out her hand and leads me through the gate and we go up the hill. We stop at two graves and I read out the death dates. They're the same. I remember what Jaci once said: *When she left she took him with her.*

"It's always there, a danger zone that can draw you in. Because you want to know, because you are compelled, because you don't understand."

"Danger of the spirit," I say, "danger of despair."

"A danger we wander into."

"Unaware of the entrapment."

"And no escape, we're captives, like Lucine in my poems."

"But who is she," I say, "who is Lucine?"

"Lucine is unimportant."

"Is she your muse?"

"Lucine brings my poems from the page to the world."

"Is it she who inspires you?"

"Lucine's the result of my poems, not the cause. I told you: I do things backwards. First the echo, the reflection; then the sound, the image."

"But is she a figment?"

"How could she be? You've seen her."

xiii

We go over the hill and the entire suburb stretches before us. It's edged by farmland, and among the houses large plots have been planted that look ready for harvest. The sun has set, and in the gathering twilight the landscape loses its doubling shadows. In the distance we can make out the ditch, the shabby little house and the junk-strewn lot beside it.

"Next stop," Jaci says.

We go down the hill, and the first field we come to blocks our way. The crop is green, rustling, taller than we are. It has a scissoring sway. We touch the serrated edges and we have to walk around. Jaci pauses, transfixed. She stares into the field and recites.

The cornfield filled with whispering
Follows us
As we skirt it,
Voices husky and the sharp stalk leaves
Keeping us from cutting through.

"Feral," Jaci says, "don't you feel it? Some runaway force hiding in there, engendered by its own sheer density, menacing, untamed and dangerous, threatening us, to keep us out, and at the same time seducing us, luring us in.

"I stood here with Tomas. He said he could hear it. Hear what? I wondered."

And now I know why we're here. The moment resonates loss—of innocence as much as the loss of her brother. It was here, with him, that the blow of mortality, that first awareness, struck her, and the total ineffectuality of trying to protect anyone from it.

I push away this chance to share my own pain, to commiserate, to console her, to weep ourselves into each other's anguish. Nothing eases my pain beyond my devotion to its intensity.

We keep our eyes on the line where tassel meets sky—golden tassel, a close horizon. Up from the field a focus of gnats rises in pestering clouds. Our breathing attracts them. By instinct we hold our breath, our hands to our faces. Then the whine of mosquitoes, needles in our flesh. And then, on cue, like summoned shadows, wings swoop in.

We watch in fascination. Back and forth above the tassels, gliding, skin stretched, wings like webbed fingers, taut, guided by echoes that we can't hear. We put our hands on our heads to cover our hair, a throwback fear, it's what we were taught.

Jaci continues her poem.

Insects catch and crowd our swollen throats
And bats are wolfing down the latest hatch.
They sortie through the swarm.
That old wives' tale stubborn as religion,
We're quick to tuck our hair up for protection.

Jaci sounds depleted, as if some other self has spoken through her. We circle back to the park. In the trees, and with the sun well down, the park is only a suggestion of shadows: swing set, seesaw, merry-go-round—and the fleeting shadows of the long-gone children who played here when the trees were first planted, when the park was new.

"Shades," Jaci says, "that disappear in the dark."

"As will—"

"But enough of this. My father's cooked dinner and wants to talk to you."

xiv

It is fish baked with dill in a mustard and mayo sauce, a bowl of brown rice, a spinach salad, peppers and onions, a side dish of melon. Jaci's father lays it out on the table.

"Something I can make without a recipe," he says. "It gives me a break. You see, I don't read Greek. But Aeschylus has been translated so many times, so many ways, and that's what I work from. I conflate the literal scholarly translations with the literary lyrical ones. In this way I make it my own."

He is beaming. I don't remember his having a beard.

"The *Oresteian Trilogy*. It's a family drama. Festering hatred, cruelties, death as the avenging instrument. But we have to let that go. The page, the law, urges us to do so. Fury, outrage, threat, savagery. What way is that? It becomes endemic, roiling these ugly passions. We need to persuade ourselves toward better behavior."

He pours the wine and holds up his glass for a nodding toast.

"And not just in the personal, as Jaci and I have experienced. Force is the weapon of those who cannot persuade. And force is not just physical. Restriction is force. Intimidation is force. Banning words to keep knowledge simple, banning words to enforce an uncomplicated story. Persuasion relies on the better idea, on the triumph of appeal over bullied insistence. The civilized life is ruled by persuasion. It is based on agreement. Our anger isn't righteous, there is no such thing. We have to yield our fury to the rule of compassionate law. That's how the trilogy ends, passionate anger giving way to compassionate reason. I am telling you this because it is something we should all be telling each other. And, as is always the case, now more than ever."

He opens his arms toward the laden table.

"I prepared the food, so I get to give the lecture. Mine is the pleasure of speaking; we all have the pleasure of hearing my voice. The world has fallen from grace into desperate ignorance. It has torn itself apart. Don't be disheartened. It has always done this. And you are not dead, like my son. The moon will guide us through the night, and as my daughter has probably told you, has probably shown you, it is sometimes still here by day. The sky keeps coming to the window, and innocent birds keep thudding against this likeness. They read the light, but only the light. We read *by* the light. We make sense of our senses. We interpret what we see. And this gives us wonder, and worry—we get both. If not, we'd be fooling ourselves. This light today touches our faces and impresses us with this memory. When the mark it has made lifts out, who knows toward what passage—or glass—those wings will fly?"

He waves us off after dinner, and Jaci takes me in her car to the house by the junk lot.

"Manifesto," she mutters, shifting a gear, "communique." I assume she is tired of the speech. "Social concerns," she says, "are not my great interest."

"But there is truth in what he says."

"Obviously."

In the poem I had seen on her desk, "the task of self" still showed through the partial erasure. When she changed it to "the task of else" she took it somewhere beyond. This is how she works. She starts with rejection and stays there until she can turn it into something she accepts. What is my duty to myself? That is her question. And by changing one word, the duty to herself becomes a duty to the world beyond herself.

Jaci parks the car. We walk over the footbridge and open the door. The room is empty except for the bed. We undress and hang our clothes in the closet. Jaci carefully pulls back the covers, we get into the bed and draw up the sheets, draw them snug. We tuck ourselves in, neatly arranged, and go to sleep.

XV

In the morning we wake to soft light. It moves slowly, and we lie there all day, hour after hour, watching the shadows. The shadows drift, shift, and we watch them change. We watch them build, then yield. We watch them recover.

The shadows merge into one, then pull apart. They gather themselves for the effort of holding, the redoubled effort of letting go. We don't know where they come from, there is nothing in the room to shape them.

The bed is soft and the mattress sags to the depth of our bodies. We keep the covers aligned, unbunched and level.

Jaci is quiet. I wait for her to recite.

The blanket we hunker
Under is heavy. We're pressed
So deep the spread covers us flat
And the bed looks made
While we are still in it.

Jaci's voice is inexpressibly sad, an oracle voice that cannot deny the future it dreads. Her smile can manage no joy. I have replaced Lucine as a prop for her poems and can't help but think of Agamemnon, the fatal blade that awaited him, a blade he deserved.

My eyes follow Jaci's to the closet. I can see our clothes through the slats in the door, ghostly white. Jaci leans to the side of the bed and I see her hand drop to the floor. I hear a click, metallic, and I'm frightened, frightened almost to the point of desire.

"Just to be clear," Jaci says.

Then from under the bed a noise of indistinct sound: music, garbled. The reception is poor, her voice barely lifting above it.

Our room is the same without us:
Empty sleeves through closet louvers,
Radio static untuning the station.
Disappearing like this we question whether
Doubt really means we exist.

I think of the sky, the cloudless sky. I think of calm sea unchanged by the cloudless sky's reflection. Jaci and I have committed ourselves to the uncommitted life. We are deep in the pit of annihilating mood, and we let ourselves sink. The bog can be only so deep. We want to know what lies at the bottom.

xvi

On the bus back to the city I have the feeling that living is over, that it will not come again, not its pain nor its beauty. I have that strange and even stranger feeling that isn't replaced by anything else. It feels like a day without weather, a void that doesn't exist.

Then the feeling slips away, and when it is gone I am utterly alone. No one on the bus is talking, and my sense of isolation rises from the streets and terrain. I think that if I could see this feeling from above, could look at the city from a bird's-eye view, I would understand how to navigate its moods, or at least understand why I am lost here.

In the evening the sky doesn't properly darken, as if some whiteness from the day refuses to be dispelled. I sense it in my bath, sunken in the tub, gazing at the skylight. No dream comes to visit. Nothing transports me.

The light is wrong, a dim glow, more than would come from the moon. It seems to be searching the panel of glass, like the beam of a flashlight, except that the light is diffuse, evenly spread, steady and constant. The skylight looks detached, no longer connected, lifted and floating.

I get out of the tub and go to the window. People are out on the street in wonder, milling about. I dress and go down and finally see it; everyone sees it. We are all looking up, all along the street.

Even Selena, her child in hand; not quite in hand, their fingertips touching. The child I saw that first day in the park. A little girl. The little girl I myself might have had, had I had a little girl. The little girl I myself might have been, had I been a little girl.

The whole neighborhood is out, looking up at the sky. I say *looking up* because no one is looking to the distance. We are all looking into the circle above us.

Some people point, though there is nothing in particular to point to, no spot different from another. It doesn't matter where we stand, it doesn't matter where we look. It is the same one place to the next.

Something coming to an end, something waiting to begin, something rare and atmospheric. At first no one is concerned, we are all already getting used to it. It's a quick accommodation, our amnesia for the normal. But this gives way to doubt, to worry, and slowly, one by one, we start to question our easy acceptance.

xvii

Night had a hold on the city, the way it pushed its moon into the day. And now it has a stranglehold, pulling the day's light into night sky. We are flirting with notions of celestial speculation that even the imagination would consider suspicious. And the city itself is at fault, because it lets itself be used. It is a pretext for supposing the far-fetched, for entertaining the improbable.

When light comes in through a pane of glass, anything can happen. It's like a pencil entering a piece of paper, making its mark. It's like taking a train. Somewhere down those parallel tracks the rails get wide, the space opens out to a view through a window. And beyond this window we drink in the sky, the cup of blue, the clouded day, let the jagged shadows, the shards of sunlight, catch in our throats as they may.

Our city rests on undisturbed land. The long gorge is still there, has never been filled, and the little hills have never been flattened. Signs mark our historic sites or the spot where the buildings once stood. Those streets are aromatic. They have a stagnant used-up smell.

On one such street a woman signals my attention. She is mouthing to me excitedly, not saying a word—her face expressive, her gesture wild, her bright lips moving without making a sound. I play along, cover my ears, palms flat to my head as if I cannot bear to hear what she is saying. She is surprised by my reaction, but immediately knows what to do. She raises a finger to her lips and holds it there, obedient, pretending to hush herself.

Nothing is familiar anymore, streets no longer recognizable. They seem to be on some slow rotation, a circling so languid it never repeats. I imagine I have made a discovery, am onto something, off the wheel and out on a tangent. I wander the city for clues.

Passing a shop I pause to take in the aquarium displayed in the window. I admire my face in the glass, my reflection superimposed on a speckled fish that rises like a bubble in the effervescent water, mute lips working an O into an oval.

Because I have stopped, someone comes up and asks for directions. She wants to get to the harbor because she has heard they sell fish there. I give the instructions carefully, repeat them slowly, repeat them again. But she doesn't pay attention, or can't, and continues on her way, more happily lost, I believe, for my effort.

The next stranger I meet I will guide to the building where I live. I will point out the shadows, gray shadows, the residual ghosts. They are only architectural ghosts—the vestige of a portico, vestige of a window: the one torn off, the other boarded over and covered with stucco, obliterated features of another time, a time more gracious in its manner of living.

I will not ask this companion to embrace the nostalgia, to succumb to a dream of the portico's shade, to indulge the voyeur's glance through the window that is no longer there. The past is a kind of solitude, and solitude is sacrosanct.

Solitude is also a psychological imperative. Just ask the ground-floor tenant in his little apartment next to the grocery. Today when I catch him inserting his key he looks at me intently, glares into my eyes so that I have to look away.

"I've lived here longer than you have."

"You would know," I say. "Why haven't we met?"

He looks at my face more closely, studying some

detail—the angle of cheek to chin, the balance of eyes to brow—then examines himself in the sheen of his door.

"There's a difference."

"What's the difference?"

"That's what I meant to say."

He has been working his key upside down. He figures this out, turns it over and asks my age. I tell him thirty-one.

"There's a difference," he says. "I'm forty. But not a young forty. I'm like the man of seventy who says he still feels as if he were forty. There's always a discrepancy, there has to be. I've been here nine years because I wanted to see what difference it would make."

He goes inside, closing the door behind him. I am not going to let him get away. He has started something, and I want him to finish it. I press the button for the doorbell.

There's a muted click. "I've disconnected it," he says through the door. "If you want to come in you'll have to knock."

xviii

Coffee, I tell myself, and a glass of wine—the comfort of habit.

Across from the Museum of Indigenous Peoples I take a long look at the steps leading up. I know I am never going to climb them. Whatever is preserved inside those doors has zero hope of revival, no chance of resurrection. The world is done with that. It is not coming back.

I pull out a chair at my usual table at the sidewalk café. Looking up I see Selena. She is wearing tall heels, a mesh bag on her shoulder. The sunshine is bright on her brow, great clarity of light. She puts on a hat with a wide white brim and her eyes stay bright in the shadow.

A stranger approaches her, and with vintage manners he doffs his fedora. He plays the sun for a trick, and the shadow of his hat, as white as a dove, flies off to the trees. "Yes, I know," the man says when they come to my table.

Memories, dreams, inspirations: they aren't stable, they don't hold. They are all abruptions, all breakaways—now visual, now notional, now oracular, now petulant.

They come in a rush, bunched, kaleidoscopic; they come in spurts, fragments, disjointed and ragged; they are sweet, bittersweet; they are revulsions or mere curiosities.

Selena reaches into her bag.

"I bought you a notebook," she says, "the brightest color they had." She pauses to keep my attention. "General nondescript gloom," she says, "if you want to know. That's what lies at the bottom. It is no more authentic than unabashed joy."

FOUR

i

The monthly checks from the insurance annuity have been more bane than boon. I've been living off her death as if Erin were still with me. I have told myself this from the start.

The money takes care of the basics, body and soul if not together at least in touch. But the money's a degenerating windfall. It lets me behave in an unengaged way, with the onlooker's license for serial living. I've been skylighting, never touching down, just passing through as if I myself were the weather.

Havana was our dream on the day we eloped, our dream of the funky tropics. We knew we'd never go there, but it wasn't the same as pretending. It was a step toward courage in defiance of behavioral control, career-track expectations.

Havana had been off limits since before we were born. Where else to excite our hearts but in a place that could never disprove us? Where else to snub our important future but in a place we could only invent?

That dream is dashed—I am beginning to see my limitations. Havana won't happen.

But neither will my exile continue. I'm done here. A news feed on my phone is my card to get out of jail free. Pastor Lorthew Lake in that Florida beach town has been arrested for having sex with a minor. It had been going on for years until he dumped her on her eighteenth birthday. The girl went public, photo and all, and the news feed gave the date for her coming of age: the very night of our encounter on the beach. My crime turned legal by the grace of one day.

And now Florida is safe, and simulation will suffice. Little Cuba—that's as close as I will get to Havana, the perfect stand-in, the Latin Quarter, Ybor City.

I book a flight to Tampa.

ii

My itinerary shows a change of planes at an airport hub. There is nothing direct because I have waited too long to buy my ticket. The layover doubles the trip's duration, but a tailwind brings me in early. The same wind delays the layover flight from the other direction. I am able to board a connecting flight hours before mine on standby status, thanks to the no-shows.

And only because the man next in line for the last open seat has a sudden attack of premonition. He decides to stick to his original booking and wait for the plane on his schedule. Some things, he says, are meant to be.

To this I reply, though he doesn't get the joke, "There are no accidents."

I have been trained as a lawyer. I repeat this phrase as mantra and in lieu of apology. If the plane is going to crash it has nothing to do with the person sitting in the reassigned seat. Though that of course is neither the point nor any reassurance. Nor, if the plane goes down, any consolation.

Each person's fate aligns with every choice we ever make, except to the extent that things cannot happen other than they do. The straight, the narrow, does not exist. And even if it does exist it is not a possibility. We cannot help but go off. Nor is this cause for concern. Divergences always lead somewhere.

iii

It's a ghostly flight, the full moon setting through the windows on one side and dawn coming into the windows on the other. My seatmate works at his laptop, eerie dull light from the screen. He is running a compilation of figures, comparing the yields of varying scenarios with color-coded columns and intersecting charts.

The light from his screen is the same as the light in my parents' bedroom the night I was drawn from my toddler bed by the sudden gasp, the muffled huff. The night I was drawn in my footie pajamas to my parents' door by the light from the TV on their dresser, volume off, their bed in shadow, the blankets humped, a clandestine chiaroscuro of movement, the glow from the screen reflecting off the wall, and like a close-up cameo in a silent film, my mother turned toward me, exposing the cratered look on her face.

I close my eyes to block this light, closed my eyes then and close them now. The memory goes away, and even the plane's cabin—its exit signs, its runner lights—disappears. I am nowhere: sky above, sky below, sky within sky, and skies all around.

But I can't block it out completely. A birthday, a picnic in a park, a cake, the right number of candles. My father says, "*Zwolf*," pronouncing the vowel wrong.

My mother corrects him. "You forgot the umlaut."

"A dozen," my father says, his smart-aleck tone.

The candles burn low, my breath is shallow. I manage to blow out eleven.

"*Elf*," my mother says. "They almost rhyme." She has taught me the word for my age each year since I entered first grade. *Sechs*, *sieben*, *acht*, *neun*, *zehn*, *elf*.

My father's attempt to teach me *twelve* feels false. Though he's learned the words she uses most often, he's picked up less of her language than I have.

But he is the one who hands me my present. It's a military watch with analogue hours. I open the band and strap it on, and I'm pleased with the way it looks on my wrist.

"One-thirty," I say, ignoring the p.m. dial.

"*Halb zwei*," my mother says. She has also been teaching me time.

iv

I don't know who to fault for the things that went

wrong between them. Sometimes the guilt, the blame for their estrangement, feels like my own. As if the balance on which they relied had been tipped too far by my presence, some stability overturned. As if I had stolen affection that rightly belonged to each other.

Our last trip Out West we had come through scrub brush and grasslands, pueblo ruins and cactus stands, crumbled towns and barren desert. It felt like an old-time cowboy movie, and each night outside our camper trailer I longed for the certainty of black-and-white. But the casino West could not be avoided. In the lit-up sky beyond our campsite we could almost hear the spin of roulette, the rattle of dice and ice cubes.

We finally went there. Las Vegas was crowded, hot, noisy and garish. My mother could not hide her disdain. She scoffed at the plaza fountain where tourists pitched coins and even my father flipped a bright quarter.

"Jackpot," he said as it hit the water.

I asked what he wished for.

"Jackpot," he said, "I wished for the jackpot."

All this water, all this splashing, all this burnt-out desert. And my mother pressing her palms together, then wedging them open, allowing whatever they held to drain out.

Days later we drove through the Petrified Forest, where fallen trees had been buried so quickly they turned into stone. On a scenic loop we stopped for the view and my mother stepped out onto parking-lot asphalt, amazed at the heat working up through her turquoise huaraches. She pulled her hand from her pocket and slowly bent down to the softened blacktop.

"My *Wunsch*," she said, "this is my *Wunsch*," pushing a penny into the tar.

Her shadow was bunched as she crouched, but as she stood up it flowed through the length of her body, her flushing face, her face turning pale; and the sweat on her arms, gleaming with light, disappeared in dry air as the moisture broke through her skin.

"If wishes were horses…" my father said.

There was something at stake in his passive gibe, his sardonic and unfinished sentence, but he let the words hang. We went back to the car and got in.

From the backseat, leaning forward between them, I could see my father's jaw clenching his teeth against anything else he might say, my mother's face slack, her breath taking place as something intensely private, a solitude, a cherished and unshared vision. She seemed to be looking into a distance that I could not see, a distance our windshield would fail to discover.

I imagined a landscape that never ended, that kept on going as long as you kept moving toward it. Or not even toward it, just moving. You could travel any direction you wanted, turn and turn again, and it would always pivot to stay in front of you.

I wanted us to go there, to heed some call away from this intractable tension that had snared their willingness to talk to one another. I had a child's belief in psychic thinking and summoned what power I could, straining my ears as if listening intently might somehow reach into their quarrel and will them to speak.

But my parents could not let go. They would not speak, they would not speak. And it wasn't something they kept to themselves—as the car started up, their silence drifted like heat itself out toward the silence around us.

We seemed to be gasping. That dangling phrase had drawn all breath from the car. *If wishes were horses*... We were stuck, nothing was moving. The wind that blew us wherever we wanted had turned itself into a net. My parents were snagged, stymied by a sentence they could not end.

"Horses would fly," I offered, to finish the sentence for them. This didn't make sense, though I knew that it did, and I slouched on the seat behind them, looking out at the scrubby terrain, desperate for hooves that might lift into air and give my words their meaning.

V

My seatmate closes his laptop, and sometime later I hear the landing gear drop. Our approach to Tampa is announced and smooth. I open my eyes to a glowing runway. We come down like a moth to a lineup of lamps. We touch the tarmac without any bounce. The plane comes to a stop and then we just sit there.

"Gate control," the pilot says on the intercom. "We'll be moving soon."

My seatmate and I exchange glances.

"At least we're on the ground."

"This makes me nervous." He is German, the accent.

"Flying?"

"Waiting."

He has come here on business, and I ask what kind. Manufacturing, he says, cosmetic devices. He works for some kind of investment group headquartered in Frankfurt. They have acquired a new company in Connecticut, are going to restructure, moving it down to the Sunshine State, "lock, stock and barrel. The whole enchilada." His smile holds back a laugh.

"The whole rifle."

He gets my joke and lets the laugh out. It is his third trip to Tampa, "scouting the terrain." I try to envision his product. All I can think of are lipstick tubes.

"Nail clippers, tweezers." He has pulled out a glossy brochure and gives me a quick tutorial: the pressing machines, the molds, the spot-welding process, the shot blasting, the blade edging and final inspection. "The quality is in the calibration," he says and points to the logo on his briefcase, a few basic lines, suggesting a stickman. "Keep it simple," he says, "that is our motto." And then as if remembering his manners he says, "What about you?"

"Compatriot." I show him my German passport.

He looks at me quizzically. "But surely not born there."

"Never been there. My mother was born there. That's why I qualified. I got it by mail."

"Oh yes," he says. "Repatriation has seen a big boom. Because now it is not just the *Vaterland.* You can go anywhere you want in the whole EU. I myself would like to live in a land where lemon trees grow."

It is the first day of Savings Time and the morning is an hour darker than the same time yesterday. He already has his sunglasses on when the plane taxis to the gate. On the tram to the terminal the sunrise clears, a real glare. I have to turn away and I see it reflected in his lenses.

"You thought I was…*jumping the gun*," he laughs, "putting these on."

His English is good, and the accent gives it precision. But his name disappoints. It's Frank, not the Gerhart or Dieter I expected. He makes up for this by the way he says mine, *Niklaus*, as if to correct me.

We duck into the men's room and stand side by side at the urinals. "What is so fascinating about this wall"—he looks over at me pretending to peek—"that we are so intent on staring at it?"

In the concourse he seems amused by the crowd, the resigned gestalt among those who are leaving compared to the excitement of those coming in. The airport's surprisingly busy for so early in the day, and another plane has landed.

"Here," he says, and gives me the stub for his luggage—"a big brown one."

He tells me to meet him at Hertz. An efficient plan: by the time I lug over his suitcase he's advanced to the front of the line.

He steps up to the counter. "Ram Big Horn," he says. "Frank Wolke."

We say goodbye in the parking garage. As I am giving my rental the once-around he hangs out his window and waves, a blast of country from his radio: *My footsteps at your fancy home, scuffed boots on polished stone.* I laugh as he sings along.

This is his own little dream, and strudel plays no part in it. "Fantasyland," he said at the counter, and I didn't need much persuading. My upgrade's a silver Mustang, white leather seats. The first thing I do is lower the blue canvas top.

The gas tank is full, and the impressive compass is pointed due west. I've pulled out of the airport and turned onto MLK Boulevard. Right direction, wrong route. I get off on Cortez, turn around and wait at the corner for the light. Top down, unroofed to the world, I hear the chirp of an osprey, melodious raptor, as sweet as a songbird, perched on the top of a lamp pole.

It all feels familiar, relaxed, arms extended to the wheel, a position embedded in my brain, in the fibers of my muscle, on hold since the accident. All is restored under the sun. The driver's side is comfortably where I remember it to be.

There once, there forever, some people believe.

Erin on the puddled streets on a drizzly day in

Donegal, in her bright yellow raincoat a half block ahead of me. She walks under a storefront awning, stepping into the shadowy light—and is instantly gone, total disappearance as I'm wiping the rain from my eyes. I hurry to the spot, she's nowhere. I look into the store, at the shelves and racks, and of course I see her—she's gone inside to look at sweaters.

There once, once only. And also again and again.

vi

I take the Dale Mabry Highway to the auxiliary interstate and cross Old Tampa Bay on the Howard Frankland Bridge, a span so long you are advised to check gas before getting on. For such wide expanse of water the bay is remarkably shallow. Long-legged birds wading from shore dot the surface like little white islands.

I drive west on Ulmerton Road, a functionary stretch that serves only the purpose of getting you through, passing by Highpoint (elevation thirteen feet) and eventually Largo. There I hit rush-hour traffic and Largo lives up to its name.

At Ridgecrest I loop south on Walsingham Road, cross the Indian Rocks Causeway to the barrier islands that run the whole length of Pinellas County. The road hooks down on Gulf Boulevard and passes through a welter of contiguous beach towns: Indian Shores, Redington Shores, Madeira Beach, and a town actually named Treasure Island.

I cross the bridge at Blind Pass to St. Pete Beach, an

island unto itself. There is a vacancy sign at the Bon-Aire Beachfront Motel. I get a room and spend the rest of the day there, a napping respite, shades drawn.

The Don CeSar is a mile further down. Frank said to meet at the Rowe Bar at seven. With the time change this makes it just before sunset. He wants to introduce me to Helles, a Tampa lager brewed the way Germans brew lager.

I picture him already there, saving me a spot for nature's diurnal dousing. He has a practiced routine from previous visits, gets a comfortable seat in the fire-pit section, where a row of low dunes obstructs the view of the horizon. He likes to sit there facing away from the water. His pleasure, he said, is to stay in his seat when everyone else stands up, eager to catch the last moments of sun.

The men stand tall and the women balance on tiptoe. They fascinate him with their mutual resolve to see over the dunes.

They seem to stand to attention, and it strikes him as a patriotic exercise, like the protocol for lowering the flag. As they strain to watch the light expire, he watches the light slip slowly out of their faces. The rising shadow engraves their faces like sculpture, like ancient carved stone serving some unpreserved purpose, monolithic statues staring into the weather that year after year has eroded all knowledge of why they are there. But the human faces do not partake. It's not awe that he sees in those faces, just a fierce determination, a chiseled desire for spectacle, and they are not going to be denied.

This is a studied watching that I know so well. The way we sat on that family trip Out West, my parents and I, when the road divided and we had to decide which way to go. But the choice was not entirely ours.

We were sitting in the car keeping close watch on a funnel. It was picking up sand in the alkaline desert, still a safe distance, but slowly advancing. Above us the sky was clear, a few clouds drifting. My father—science teacher's holiday—said that the light that entered those clouds was scattered, that's why they were white.

"Scattering," he said, "is also what makes the sky blue."

I didn't understand how a single cause could produce two different effects. My mother also had doubts. "Scattering," she said, as if the word were new to her.

Between our car and the funnel was the relic of a drive-in theater, overgrown, weedy, the concession stand boarded, the screen like an empty billboard—and brilliantly white. My mother pointed this out. "The sky," she said, "is blue because endless, nothing gets past."

The road had forked by a last-chance signpost—last chance for something that was dangling and faded, I couldn't read what. We were waiting to see which path the storm took before choosing our direction. Without pulling over we had stopped in our lane, there were no other cars.

"Not a tornado," my father said. "It's only a twister."

The funnel was starting to fatten, the distance closing. But outside our car the air was calm, and on the road in front of us a tumbleweed ambled across our lane, paused, then slowly rolled off to the other side. Our windows were open, I felt the changed pressure. As the funnel approached, dark birds shot up and flew toward us.

"That means we're safe right here, if they're coming this way."

"Those aren't birds."

We closed our windows as the wind came down and slapped us. On either side, pieces of shingle torn from the drive-in's snack bar flew by our car without touching it. In the funnel itself darker debris was coming right at us. Instead of taking the road going left or the road going right my father shifted to reverse and turned the car around.

vii

My room at the Bon-Aire Beachfront Motel faces onto a courtyard at the furthest end, and when I open the door I hear the soft lap, the hollow dull flop of calmed waves. I put on my jacket and walk past the row of thick potted plants. They have a variegated leaf and look so exotic I take them at first to be plastic.

A low brick sea wall divides the pavement from the sand. With a small step down I go out the passthrough. Stray gulls fly by, trotting the air like town dogs. Then the sky is filled with dozens of gulls as if the wind has caught the whole flock in a current. They swirl in gray spirals, bunched like litter, then disperse and bunch once again.

The breeze lifts, the temperature drops, and I put up my collar. The wall has a capstone the height of a bench. I sit down and zip my jacket. Out on the Gulf the water's curve meets the undefined sky. Blue sea and blue sky, a color that water cannot absorb, a color the atmosphere scatters.

I hold up my hand and measure the gap between sun and horizon. Two fingers mean thirty more minutes till sunset. I am eager to see it—the flash, of all colors green, if conditions are right, as the rim of the sun drops out of sight.

"Some times of day don't show themselves direct, they're just reflected on." Erin says this dreamily. She means reflected on the surface, as if the day were a pond and these moments are creatures slipping down for a drink. Their reflections ripple as they lap, indistinct the instant we see them. "Some times of day only follow on their memory, don't happen till they're past." We are standing on a hill, halfway up in tangled grass. We watch the sun going down, it drops quickly, the shadows getting longer. We're swallowed by shadow, shadows all around us—the sun has set. Then we climb the hill and watch it set again.

I am not going to keep my rendezvous with Frank. Too many plans have been altered, too many random events—the indirect flight, the tailwind, the no-show at the airport hub—led to our traveling as seatmates.

Random occurrence is something we all have to live with, but this would be pushing it a little too far. Because Frank has an aunt in Sarasota, forty miles down the coast, whom he plans to visit at the tiki bar she runs with her husband. "Second husband," Frank said, "her old flame." The odds are against it, but the odds are starting to stack.

Sarasota is where my father met my mother. And that's where she went when she left us. The man who'd been her lover still lived there. Frank was from Hanover, and my mother used to joke about the "wurst town," Braunschweig, where she had grown up. Same state. Frank's aunt and my mother…there's a chance they are one and the same.

After my mother left us, and when my father told me I wasn't his son, I embraced the new feeling of absolute loneness as if it were a birthright. I felt like an orphan, free to break off the stultifying influence of family. This severance—her leaving, his telling me the tale of my bastardy—and the modest inheritance he surprisingly left me, were a boon to my freedom. I am not going to sabotage the gift they gave me by stumbling upon a long-lost parent.

There was a time when I thought those childhood trips, the roads we traveled together, would fulfill their promise, would carry us into a happy future. Not just the sights but even the sound, the light-footed thump of a cat jumping down off a porch rail, the brindled cat that slipped through the screen door at the desert roadside grocery we stopped at for sodas; and bought candy bars too, Payday, since nuts wouldn't melt and would replenish lost salt. We'd had a long drive and were feeling road-giddy. They tossed their wrappers to the back and I batted them down, goal tender of the windows. "Good save!" my father shouted, his words wobbled by wind; and my mother, "Jesus saves!" a call and response, shouting out the big words on a billboard.

That moment of joy, of feeling like family, was brief, and I am hard-pressed to think of another. If it hadn't happened I might not have known what I was missing.

The sunbeam glistens on the Gulf, and now the sun touches, orb on water. I am keeping a safe watch, glancing at it, blinking, looking away. Then glancing again, the way my mother taught me. Our eyes don't always know what harms them. We can't always look at the thing we most want to see.

With the last of the light the gulls have settled, bedding down in the sand. The top rim of the sun lowers to the edge of sky and water. Hold steady, I tell myself, these last few seconds, don't look away till it's gone, blink and you will miss it. Wait for the flash, if it comes. Keep your eyes open.

I obey myself and get my wish. Not the wow, not the neon gleam of bright explosion—just the pastel, the sudden glow, the soft green arc slipping out of the spectrum, extinguished the moment it's lit.

viii

What I see in the sky are Erin's memories. They have folded into mine and I assume them as my own. I hold her memories in trust, I am their sole depository.

A church half empty, but crowded up front. Erin in back. In vicarious recollection I am there. She listens to the muffled talk, the handkerchiefed coughs that ascend toward the ceiling, the high vault. A kind of contagion: I feel hoarse without speaking.

Erin has come here alone, and in this memory I have taken as my own I am subsumed in her solitude. All day a low cloud has hung from the sky, dense fabric in the air, a curtain on the sun. The stained glass is dim, as if purposely so. She can hear as if standing next to them a sacristan telling an altar boy that the only lighting is to come from the candles.

The pew she sits on is trimmed at just the right cut to pinch at the knees. Erin's palming the bench. Her fingers caress the honey-brown grain where it swells to a curve. She feels the worn pine press into her flesh the gloss of a hundred years, the rubbed-in sheen from a century of buttocks in trousers and skirts sliding over this varnish.

I am Erin, I sit here alone. My pronouns are she and I. At twenty years of age she cannot sit in church without remembering having sat there as a girl. Religion had been the pool I stared into, where I'd seen my own beauty shimmering on the surface. I cannot imagine myself living and dying and the world continuing on as if nothing much had happened.

Almost to her teens Erin believed that the life of this world had nowhere else to go once it had come to her. She'd been comforted by this sense of culmination. She had no doubt that the final reckoning would occur within her lifetime and call all creation to account.

In adolescence she developed a contrariety. She rejected comfort and inclusion and did not like her thoughts to get too cozy. Being called to the bosom of God struck her as a coddling she had finally outgrown.

She believed that she could will herself exempt, that by some studied practice of abnegation the great day of judgment would take place without her.

Erin slips away when the service is over. I am her shadow. We wander to the basement and surface again along narrow stairs through a door that opens behind the altarpiece. It's a tiny space, in the front peak of the chancel. I am beside her, I become her. We catch a scent of snuffed wick, of wax, a lingering but wholly secular gloom, an air of abandoned chaos.

She did not expect the altarpiece to have so unadorned a backside. It is fixed to an anchored-on scaffold whose vertical bars and turned-out platforms contrive a mishmash of rubble and rust, inviting a climb. She can see the way up, the handholds and footholds.

She pictures a god's-eye view of the dusky nave, her cheek pressed up to the cheek of Jesus, poking her head from behind the hanging figure. But instead of climbing, I just peek out between the altarpiece and the wall. I feel like a child whose naughtiness is so close to behaving that no one can scold him.

It's a narrow fit, head only, and Erin's shoulders are scrunched. When she raises her head the dimness dispels: the windows flare with sudden sunshine and the church is bathed in a glimmering fest, a hosanna of light. The idea of glory is golden, it seems to hover; it is there for her to touch.

She cranes her neck and lifts her eyes toward the glowing height of the altarpiece. The dark wood gleams with tropical pigment, the polished mahogany against her cheek surging with the energy of sap and photosynthesis, the crown of this tree rising out of its forest and spreading its leaves to the pull of light, the flap and squawk of toucans and macaws, the momentary vision of paradisiacal canopies.

Erin pulls her head back and drops to her knees in the dust behind the altarpiece, and there she presses her palms together on the impulse of prayer. I do the same. But all we can manage is to fold our fingers inward, forming this-is-the-church, pop the index fingers up for this-is-the-steeple.

Erin opens her hands and looks at the people her fingers represent. They have gloss on their nails and a rounded manicure. One has a sliver of thistle under the cuticle. Other than that they all look the same, like birds in a cage. She wiggles them, prettily. Then she unclasps her hands and sets them free.

FIVE

i

The next couple of days are cloudy—no more sunsets, no more sun-setters watching for the flash. I go to Busch Gardens to see the giraffes, to Steinbrenner Field for a pre-season game between the Yankees and the Braves, to Ybor City for a sugared espresso in the shade of a wrought-iron balcony.

At the Dali Museum the landscapes are playfully eerie, a phantasma of fragmented psyche, the watches like melted memories. I touch every instinct inside me, indulge the nude boys, the lush unapproachable women, the milk-themed surealities.

A watercolor keeps calling me back—figures of smoke, fog, wispy and disintegrating even as they form. They ascend the paper in shades of washed brown, bodies morphing into spirit, earth lifting into sky. The surrendered soul feeling its way to whatever salvation awaits it.

The middle of the week I set out to pay homage to the place where I was born. If it really is true that we steer our own lives down the road of free will, if we really arrive where the forks of our many decisions have led us, I want to trace myself back to where the other choices still had a chance.

It was there that my parents met and got married. And then I came along, a few months later. They moved north within the year so my father could finish his degree. He taught high-school science and my mother didn't love him. That lasted twelve years.

Disappointment—after my mother left us, this was our dominant feeling, my father and I toward each other. The perverse integrity of our bond would not allow us to hide it. My second year of college he announced he had stage-four cancer. He was afraid he would die near midnight, and one moment before or one moment after would make all the difference. He wanted me there to pinpoint the time, a vigil at bedside. The accuracy of his headstone depended on it.

My inheritance, he said, would be small, but enough to finish college and grad school if that was what I wanted. It was not lovingly bestowed. We had come too far under separate skies to summon the needed affection. Death scowl, that's how I would describe his expression.

He cleared his throat, an awful hacking of phlegm and dry air. He was struggling for breath but refused further treatment. I admired his obstinate will. And I also kept an eye on the clock, since that was what I was there for.

"I have something to say to you."

His voice was dysphonic, strangled and breathy. An apology would have been out of character, and in this he did not disappoint—no conversion on the death-bed. My father wasn't worried about the things I begrudged him: the harshness, the stingy withholding, the episode of violence. He believed that all his life he'd been wronged, falsely accused, unjustly dealt with and forever misunderstood. He wanted me to know this. "And," he said, "something else you should know, your mother's little secret."

It was just before midnight. If my father was going to die on October twenty-first he had twenty-four hours to do so. I should have been mourning his loss, but after what he told me I was mourning the loss of my identity.

ii

I drive down on the Tamiami Trail, through Bradenton and Whitfield, and into Sarasota, the former winter quarters for Ringling's circus. It takes me past Ringling's mansion, then down to the John Ringling Boulevard, crossing the bay on the John Ringling Causeway.

On Lido Key I book a room at the Holiday Inn, fifth-floor. It is midafternoon, and I put off unpacking till later. My window looks over the street to the Gulf. I lay a pencil on the sill and stand my new notebook beside it, its bright yellow cover leaning on the glass.

Ten minutes later I have crossed the street and am standing on the shore looking back at the notebook in the window. One hundred sheets, two hundred pages if I count both sides, the notebook I have come here to fill. From my angle below it, or because of the rail, the notebook looks foreshortened. That takes some solemnity out of the project.

The sun has warmed over the past few days, and walking bareback along shore I can feel its soft burn on my skin. Micro-damage, we are told, but to me the sun feels benevolent, like a healing, a laying-on of hands. It feels like a cure, hot fingers digging restorative touch into my body, kneading their heat through sinew and muscle, probing the bone.

The water is sparkly, the Gulf calm. Black skimmers are gliding close to the surface, living up to their name, their lowered beaks trawling.

The tide is in, the sandbars are covered, and in the shallows the water is milky, a milky tan. Close to the bottom a large dark shape, lying parallel to shore, holds its place without moving. It is twenty feet out—a shark—and a small crowd has gathered to see it.

"He just sits there," a woman says.

Another woman says, "He's not even moving."

"He's gulped air," a man says. "That's what they do. It makes his weight the same as the water. He doesn't *have* to move."

"Someone should catch him."

"Sand shark," the man says. "They're protected."

I turn toward him. "Why's that?"

The tide is fully in, and the ebb has not yet started. The water is slack, unstressed, no stream, no current. As he and I stand there facing each other, time itself goes slack; I cannot feel its flow.

His jaw drops.

"Nacht!" he says, with a look of love and anguish.

A chill, in all this heat. I can feel the cold blood. He is studying my chest, looks at my face and shakes his head, shakes his head and slowly reconsiders.

"No, of course not. But I knew a guy, same tattoo. Like thirty years ago. I've never seen another like it."

So this is the man. I know it at once. My dead father's age, as of course he would be, my father's tattoo still fixed in his mind.

I take stock of this man as if I am taking stock of myself. He has an unembarrassed body, weathered, but still holding the force of a man in his prime. It's a body full of sun, he wears flowered trunks. He has the build of a man whose strength doesn't focus on any one muscle.

"A low reproductive rate," he says, "that's why. And because they're overfished."

"But people swim here," the first woman says.

"They're not usually dangerous."

His hair is a length he must have never grown tired of, a summer blond judging by the darker sideburns. His eyes look smarter than his face, the skin on his cheeks like a draw-string pouch drawn tight.

"Nacht," he says again, and I can feel the affection.

Can feel and reject it. I don't want the emotion, don't want any part of it. I want things to make sense, to add up, to equal the whole, and most of all to leave me alone. I want the past to stop being so desperately important. Whatever he knows I want to stop him from telling me.

"Lido Beach," I say. "That's redundant. Doesn't 'lido' *mean* 'beach'?"

Recognition in his eyes, moving to his lips.

"It does," he says, "but we don't know that."

iii

Clayton Kydd came to Florida from Illinois: not, as he says, the Land-of-Lincoln Illinois, but the Wild-Bill-Hickock Illinois. He grew up in Troy Grove, the gunslinger's birthplace.

"Not much of a town," he says, "grain elevator, hardware store. So like Wild Bill I like to say from outside of Troy Grove. And like him, on a farm. Bill went west because of some trouble he got into, and I went south because of a thing called winter."

The shark has swum off and we are walking down the beach toward the other end. Clay is telling me his story, *our* story, as he puts it, though he doesn't say what he means by that.

There is a jetty of riprap abutting a clump of seagrape trees. A trodden path through the growth leads to the rows of lounges outside the Lido Resort. Two young men come out the gate, one with a child in his arms, one holding a child's hand. We catch the gate on the swing-back, before it can lock, and enter the fenced enclosure. The pool is shaped like a sock, the surrounding tables shaded by canvas umbrellas, drinks on the tables garnished with paper umbrellas in plastic cups.

"I'm a stool-man myself," Clay says, and we sit at the thatch-roofed bar. The bartender looks up from the blender, juggling three limes. Clay raises two fingers. "I'm taking the liberty to order for you. Best margaritas in town."

"So you came to Florida on a whim," I say, "but why Sarasota?"

"Serendipity. Nacht's word. I had no real plan, just a map with those Italian towns down the coast, Venice and Naples. That got my attention. But…Sarasota. I decided that Spanish was good enough, and the beaches here are *primo*."

The drinks arrive: rocks, salt—no tab, they aren't rung up.

"Nacht and I could never figure out who got here first. Couldn't figure it out because time was a little fluky back then. That wasn't his fault, he knew the actual date he arrived. I was the one who wasn't keeping records. Not even tracking the day of the week, didn't think it really mattered."

I point to his wrist. "You've come a long way, now you wear a watch."

"Her gift," he says, and laughs. "It's about time, if you get my meaning."

"I get your meaning."

"Nacht and I bonded, as they say, comparing barns: red where he grew up, white in my neck of the prairie. We also had silica in common. He had a couple of years college, I guess he was taking a break. But he was always teaching, couldn't say anything without it being some kind of lesson. Which was fine by me. I was smart, willing to learn, and he had the education."

"He had the education, but now you've got his wife."

"What I've got is my wife. They divorced."

"She told my father I wasn't his son."

"I know she did."

"That was cruel, even if true."

"Hard to take, even if it isn't."

"But is it true?"

"Nacht and me, our dots really connected. We formed a straight line. You know how *therefore* is rendered in logic, when you've got A and B and therefore C? Three dots, and if you connect them you've got yourself a triangle. Nacht taught me that. 'Ergo,' he said, and it was. It was a logical consequence, when your mother showed up."

"She told me she came over as a maid."

"Au pair, they called it. Nacht met her first, and that was the problem, because she ended up liking me better."

"So is it true?"

"You want to know if I slept with her?"

"Could there have been anyone else?"

"No. That I can tell you for sure."

"So, are you…the father?"

"I don't think that matters anymore."

"He thought you are."

"You've never been a parent. She told him that because she wanted to take you with her. He was just as cruel, not letting her do it. He was a decent guy, but easily hurt. I think his years going to school and then teaching school might have stunted him."

"You were supposed to be his friend, that straight line where your dots connected. What about that?"

"Nacht was an interesting guy, but he didn't have the knack, if you know what I mean. He was a complicated guy, beyond everyone else in a lot of ways, but never beyond his own self, so he couldn't give people what they needed, he couldn't bridge the gap."

"He's the one who ended up with her, at least at first."

"She got pregnant, she was his girlfriend, they got married. For all he knew it was his. He took her home to Wisconsin. She tried, but she wasn't into it. Twelve years was all she could manage."

"And then out of the blue…"

"Not exactly. She was taking a big chance, coming down here when she left him. I was easy to find, since we'd always kept in touch, all three of us—postcards, birthday cards, nothing flirty. But twelve years! Chemistry's volatile, that's what makes a battery work. The charge might have run down, it had been a long time. But I knew it the minute I saw her, hugged her, held her. I wanted that skin."

We sit in silence, sipping our drinks. The bartender brings over a bowl of mixed nuts, and Clay very methodically picks out the macadamias.

"Salt," he says. "You can lick it from the rim of your glass, you can suck it from these nuggets off a tree, you can wade out from shore and swim in it. Maybe now's the time to make amends. I can take you to her."

"No thanks."

"'To understand is to be free.' I read that once."

"Spinoza. Nice motto, but I've been free of this a long time."

"*Wasserhimmel*."

"You speak German?"

"It's a word she uses."

"Sky water. But what does it mean?"

"I don't know. But I guess it means, well, you've seen the sky reflected on water. This is the flip, a reflection of the sea in the sky. So there's the sky lighting the world with the world's own image. What happens here affects the heavens, maybe even realigns the stars. So that frees us to think about the world another way."

"Like how?"

"Like how some idea of a god, maybe, would see us. And that maybe it wouldn't be any different from how we see ourselves. Something like that. You should be telling me. You're the one who majored in philosophy."

"How do you know that?"

"She told me."

"How did she know?"

"There was still some contact between them. He couldn't afford your tuition, but they had an agreement—no contact between her and the boy."

"He'd only take her money on those terms?"

"For when he was dead, part of the agreement. A modest estate, as he called it, but you'd be the sole heir. On condition she never got in touch with you."

"But then he died, I had the money. He couldn't take it back. And still she didn't—"

"She didn't know right away, that he died, and even once she did she wouldn't renege. She knew you'd have enough to see you through your education."

"That's one way to justify it."

"She has a lot of integrity."

"That's way too much. Certainly more than I have."

"You've still got time." He pointedly looks at his watch. "You should see her. There must be something you want to know."

"What about her promise, about not making contact?"

"That's for her to keep, doesn't apply to you."

"Actually there isn't."

"Isn't what?"

"Anything I want to know. But tell her."

"Tell her?"

"Tell her I came into the house at suppertime and nothing was cooking. Light was filling the kitchen but the air was empty: there wasn't any ticking. Her Bavarian clock was silent. She hadn't pulled the weights like she always did at noon to rewind it, they hung all the way to the floor. The pendulum had stopped, I looked at my watch, the bird wasn't coming out. Tell her I called for her, but I called only once. My own voice scared me. It was the first time I heard my voice when no one else was there."

I slide off the stool and take out my wallet. "Let me pay for the drinks."

"Not on my turf," he says, and then: "Is there any resemblance?"

I look at his face; he stares into mine.

"I don't know. Why didn't she have a test?"

"Tests weren't so reliable back then, I don't think, the way they are now. And besides, what if he submitted the blood, or the saliva, or whatever they used, and then found out the child was actually his—kind of dumb to torpedo the marriage from the start by casting that doubt."

"I keep saying *the father*, and you keep saying *the child*."

"I know, it's strange. We're talking about *your* father, talking about *you*. Back then we weren't. You didn't exist. The world before you were born will always be a mystery. It has to be. But in the hereafter, when there aren't any secrets anymore, I wouldn't want you to find out that I lied to you."

iv

In the morning I buckle the straps on my briefcase, roll up my clothes and put them into my backpack. But there is suddenly nothing to do, and nowhere further to go.

I put my clothes back into the closet and drawers, take my notebook out of my briefcase and stand it again on the sill. For the first time I feel homeless. Not only is there nowhere to go, there is also nowhere to stay.

I feel deflated, as if the clouds have gone flat. I have abandoned my known self. Who I am now is only a stranger, my nerves unpredictable. How is it possible not to know how to live?

The sky keeps coming to the window with open invitation. I have a yellow notebook with not a mark in it. Have I lived myself into a corner?

How except by waiting it out do I get to tomorrow from today? As I begin to write this, an apprenticeship comes to an end.

Havana, that old dream, the thrill and uncertainty, the notion that Erin and I once had—idyllic, fanciful, nothing like what it surely must be. A disappointment I am ready for.

I find the googled address and turn in by the sign on a worn metal post: *WAKE'S PIERS*. A backwater marina with a gravel drive that's soft and swampy, what amounts to a fiberglass junkyard. I'm surrounded by mangroves, pelicans sitting atop the thick trees like oversized songbirds.

The boats are in drydock for bottom paint, for engine repair, for upgraded rigging. Some can be bought for the unpaid storage. They're on jack stands, covered with tarps, FOR SALE signs taped to their sterns.

I poke around, do the tap test on the deck and the hull, find the boat that suits me: no soft spots, no delamination; twenty-six feet overall, twenty at the waterline. A stern-mounted rudder, a four-foot draft, decent sails and a working windvane. A history of coastal cruising, well-equipped. It has the necessary charts, a small wooden pram.

The transaction's quick and simple. I stock the boat with rice cakes, soy nuts and tinned sardines, wasabi peas, a bag of oranges, baby carrots, and gallons and gallons of water. On a whim I add licorice and root beer, two old favorites.

On the day I set out the wind's from the east. My tack's a beam reach and I'm doing four knots. It's a comfortable heel, ten degrees, full sail.

Cuba is still off-limits, but I reject the restriction. Our Coast Guard, I am told, will try to intercept me. But there is nothing they can do. I'm traveling under my German passport, and they have no authority to turn me around.

I am making good time. The wind has veered to the south, swinging southwest, and the light is starting to fade. I'm on a starboard tack, and though the wind is light I reef my sail for safety in the dark: dark sea, dark sky. The boat glides on. With shortened sail as the night turns black I now see the moon, half of it filled with light.

Erin and I eloped in a sultry dream. Our marriage gave me confidence. But since her death I have lived like a coward, I've been clouded by hopelessness, unfaithful to both of us. The marriage vow that must not be broken is the promise to live without fear.

Book Club Questions

1. To what extent are the women Nick encounters psychological substitutes for his lost wife and estranged mother; to what extent is Nick aware of any such substitution?

2. Does your opinion of Nick change when the girl he had sex with on the beach later tells him she's underage; does your opinion change when you subsequently learn that the girl was not underage?

3. To what extent do the people Nick encounters reflect Nick's emotional and philosophical uncertainties; to what extent does he absorb theirs?

4. Why does Nick decline a reconciliation with his mother; is his decision based on strength or weakness?

5. To what extent does "serial living" free Nick for a greater openness toward his experiences; to what extent does it enable him to escape accountability for his behavior?

Gratitude

The author wishes to thank the entire production team at Regal House Publishing for the very professional manner in which they brought this book to print, with special thanks to Jaynie Royal for accepting the author's vision of what this book should be.

Acknowledgments

Portions of this work appeared in various form in the following publications: *The Best Small Fictions 2016* (Queen's Ferry Press, 2016), *Borfski Press Magazine*, *Chrysanthemum* (Austria, with German translation), *Contemporary Haibun Online*, *Crack the Spine*, *Dover Beach and My Backyard* (British Haiku Society, 2007), *Frogpond*, *Haibun Today*, *Helen Literary Magazine*, *Journeys 2017* (India), *KYSO Flash*, *KYSO Flash Anthology* (Queen's Ferry Press, 2015), *Ladybug on the Odometer* (Green Fuse Press, 2011), *The Loneliness Jacket* (Apprentice House, 2010), *LYNX*, *Modern Haibun & Tanka Prose*, *Poem of the Ahead Places* (Kattywompus Press, 2013), *The Prose Poem Project*, *River Poets Journal*, *Serving House Journal*, *Short Tale 100*, *Star 82 Review*, *Stylus* (Australia), and *Wild Goose Poetry Review*.